Book Three

Tame
ME

JENNI
BRADLEY

TAME ME
MIDWEST SERIES BOOK 3
Published by JENNI BRADLEY
Copyright © 2017 by JENNI BRADLEY
978-0-9966838-3-8

This is a work of fiction. Names, characters, places and incidents are either the product of the author's imagination or are used fictitiously, and any resemblance to actual persons, living or dead, business establishments, events or locales is entirely coincidental.

Printed in the USA.

Cover Design and Interior Format
© KILLION
THE GROUP INC.

For Rob, who has fought for our country and still manages to find humor in life. Thank you for bringing laughter and sincerity into mine.

For Liz, who has been my best friend since childhood and still chooses to keep me around.

For Abigail, who was taken from us too early. I know you are behind those pearly gates, stirring the pot and enjoying every minute of it. You are loved and missed by so many.

ACKNOWLEDGMENTS

Thank you to all of my family and friends who continuously encourage me to do what I love. A huge thank-you to all of my beta readers: my mom, Kim H., Kelly W., Jenn M., Erin F., Liz L., Chad W., Iris S., Bill S., Mike T., and Melissa L. A special thank-you to Kim H., for pushing me to produce books for her to read. This book wouldn't be as entertaining without all of your input. Thank you to my editor, Faith Williams, for making this book a smoother read. Thank you to the Killion Group for formatting, designing the cover, and helping to publish it properly.

I'd like to thank all of my readers for taking the time to read, send me feedback, and post reviews. Without you, they are just words on a page. Thank you very much for being an essential part of my journey.

PROLOGUE

I SLAMMED MY MOUTH SHUT AS the desert kicked up a sandstorm of epic proportions. I could feel the tiny particles settle between my molars. If I tightened my jaw any more, the granules would scrape off the enamel from my teeth. The desert sand surrounded my body, chafing the exposed skin as though it were a block of wood to be shaped. I peered over the skyline at the impending storm. The gigantic wall of sand could be seen for miles. In another fifteen minutes, I would lose the remainder of daylight. If I didn't get ahead of the storm, I would be trapped in this godforsaken desert for at least another twenty-four hours. That would suck major monkey balls. I needed to reevaluate my job. My body didn't perform like it used to. *For the love of Pete, my knees cracked every time I bent down!* Next thing you know, I'll be broadcasting my position to my targets. *Ugh.*

I shook my head, dislodging my unpleasant future. I had to get my head in the game. I regulated my breathing: breathe in, one-two-three; and breathe out, one-two-three. I switched the safety off and made sure my finger was light on the trigger and my eyes were open, looking through the scope. As my escape window got smaller, the intended target strolled into my line of vision.

The wind had kicked up. The dark fabric billowed around his whole body, severely distorting the outline of his frame. The sandstorm made it difficult to target a deadly body shot. An impossible shot, if you were an amateur. An amateur I most certainly wasn't. The white turban he wore around his head glowed and presented me with a beautiful shot. I inhaled, with my finger gently touching the trigger. I pulled the trigger back as I exhaled. After the shot, I relaxed my shoulder, allowing it to take the impact of my M24 SWS kickback. I remained in statuesque position until I could confirm my kill.

One minute, the man stood, talking to his minions. The next, his head tossed back as though he were in the midst of hilarity. Instead of a bullet puncturing his delicate skull. Through my scope, I witnessed the immediate moment when his life ceased. I smiled sadistically to myself as I crept from my hiding spot.

I had positioned myself far enough away that his goons would never know where the shot had come from. They would scramble around like ants rebuilding after a petulant child stomped all over their colony. Another mission completed. I relayed the time of death to my boss and logged on to my Swiss bank account. Right on time. The deposit had gone through and I got the fuck out of the devil's ass crack.

MACK 1

I HAD FINISHED SERVING MY BELOVED country as a sniper in the Army many years ago. I spent last of my career honing my skills. I enlisted and began in infantry, learning the brass tacks of combat missions. My only goal was to be a part of the backbone of the Army. I wanted to belong to this tight-knit group of men who defended our freedoms. We were trusted to capture and destroy our enemies.

I spent the bulk of my military occupational status in the infantry. The brotherhood of the Army was what kept me enlisted for so long. Having each other's back was a major understatement. It went way deeper than that. We bled for one another. We sacrificed our lives for our brother's. Some of the best men I had enlisted with were no longer here. Every one of them remained forever engraved in my heart, much like the engraving on each of those tombstones.

Partly through my career, I was selected into the highest honored program. There are only two ways to get in to the Drill Sergeant School: volunteer or be selected. Volunteering does not guarantee you a spot. I was selected for the role and I humbly accepted. Most civilians view drill sergeants as explosive officers who yell and denounce their recruits like they do in the movie

Full Metal Jacket. That is not entirely the truth. It's an extremely selective group of officers, held to the highest degree, and we hold a master knowledge of basic combat training. I mean, we were loud, pretending to be pissed off all the time, but never degrading. God, I loved commanding those soft pricks. It was tough to be that way from dawn until my men hit the barracks at night. However, there was always one asshole who would piss me off for real.

I spent three years instilling values and warrior ethos into those recruits. I felt as though I were a mother teaching a child to dress properly. I was prideful when I watched those kids graduate, believing that each and every one of them carried their pride high and had a sense of direction. After that, I went through sniper training and spent the last couple of years of my career picking off scumbags. The price on my head had increased exponentially every day. After my last tour, I had enough and wanted out.

The ironic thing was that I still picked off the leeches of the world, only in a different capacity. My buddy, Forrest, introduced me to some high-profile people who needed some nasty individuals extinguished. For all intents and purposes, I was a ghost. The men who employed me could never be traced back to me. Forrest worked protection detail for many of the individuals who hired me, and I did their dirty work.

A buddy of mine had introduced me to Forrest when I was stationed in California. We had hit it off and became friends. I have since lost contact with him. He appeared to have dissolved into thin air. Last I heard, one of the guys he was protecting actually used his youngest daughter as a human shield during a scuffle. Forrest tried to intervene and take the girl away but it was too late. I had also heard that he went bat-shit crazy, quickly snuff-ing out the guy who fired the shot and then snapped the neck of the guy he was supposed to be protecting. From that moment on, he left and I haven't heard where he had resurfaced, if at all.

Since leaving the military, my moral compass had skewed slightly. It became ridiculously tiresome trying to live the life of a civilian. Within six months, civilian life proved to be an unstable and chaotic environment for me. I needed to return to the only thing that I knew how to do. However, this time I had the freedom to choose the assignments. A mark is a mark to me, as long as I got paid well to do the hit. I value life but in my line of work, all of my marks deserved more than an easy bullet through the head. I'm not there to dole out pun-ishment, only to send them to their maker faster so that he can finish the job.

Darkness shrouded every corner of the room. I sat there, numb––more like trying for numbness. It was my way of decompressing after a mission. It's not that I hated my job; for the most part, it was incredible, especially for an adrenaline junkie like me. I got to utilize my exper-tise that I had learned from my stint in the Army as well as send some sleazy motherfuckers to hell. When it's my time to clock out, I'll be right down there with them too. My mind was as sharp as a cactus thorn but my body was as exhausted as a hyper-vigilant mother.

I'm no saint nor would I ever claim to be. I'd say I closed my eyes for the sandman but I slept with them wide open. I found it easier to catch my enemies off guard and it really mind-fucked my squad. They never knew when I was sleeping or awake. I made it damn hard for them to pull a prank on me. As I started to nod off the shrill of my cell pulled me back to the darkened room. I debated on answering it. Not many people had my personal number and the ones who did were important to me, almost as though they were family.

"Yeah," I grumbled.

"Hey, Mack, how you been? You back on home soil yet?"

"Forrest, you fucker! I'm still finding sand in places where it shouldn't be. What a shit hole. I'm flying high, enjoying my free time before my next job. How the fuck are you? Heard you walked away after your last assignment." Elation hit exhaustion out of the park after I heard my friend's voice.

"Fuck, I had to, man. I'd seen too much disturbing shit. It was getting too dark for my blood. It's all—good, though. I'm going to start up my own security business. When you're ready, I want you on my team."

"Will do. As much as I'd love to reminisce with you, I'm sure this isn't a social call." I chuckled at my own joke.

"I need you to locate a Eugene Launer. Then, I need you to find all the information you can on him. I want habits, financial status, friends, etc. Hell, I want to know which hand he wipes his ass with. If you can find it, then I want it," he said, getting right to the point.

"Do I want to know why I am collecting this intel for you?" I was only mildly curious as to why he wanted it.

"I'll tell you later," he answered in a cavalier tone.

For Forrest, I would get him what he needed regardless whether I ever knew the specifics. Forrest was the epitome of a good guy. He didn't have a mean bone in his body. That's why he chose to protect high-profile people, whereas I did their dirty bidding. That's why I knew he needed my help. If he called me, it was due to his conscience eating at him. He'd want to bring in a deal-closer, one who, if need be, could finish the job and he would have clean hands and a clear mind.

"Am I going to get a call to help with removal?" There was an underlying seriousness to my voice. I liked to be informed of that beforehand, not that it mattered one way or the other.

"Maybe," he growled into the phone.

"All right. I'll get you the info as soon as I have it."

"Thanks. Talk to you soon."

With my motor firing on all cylinders, sleep was the last thing that I would accomplish for the foreseeable future. I slammed the recliner back in place and rocked myself out of the chair. I stretched my limbs and listened to the pops and cracks of my joints as I loosened my muscles. *Fuck, I felt old.*

I plopped in the worn chair at the kitchen table where my laptop sat. Pulled up a quick search of Eugene. A bunch of hits popped up but most of them didn't pertain to this particular character. The one article that did catch my eye was the arrest record for domestic violence. *Interesting. Looks like we have a seedy winner— ding, ding, ding.* Now that my interest had been piqued, I let the researching begin. I pulled the tab on my frosty Coors Light and guzzled half of it down before I zeroed in on my next target.

Forrest hadn't given me much to go on and of course the standard Internet search wouldn't yield what I really wanted to know. I managed to slip in the back door of the virtual world and started my favorite game of cat and mouse. I rubbed my hands together maniacally and gleefully gathered every little bit of dirt I could on this guy. When my eyes began to cross from the hours in front of the bright screen, I shut it down and went back to my recliner. I clicked on the TV for background noise and dove into a murky pool of dreamless sleep.

I spent the next couple of days collecting information. I put the data on a thumb drive and booked a seat on the next plane out to the land of cornfields. I wanted to personally deliver the drive. I wouldn't call Indiana my retirement state but for a quick trip to catch up with a good buddy and the possibility for bloodshed—well, count me in. I'd stay until the job was finished. No matter how long it took. Our loyalty for each other didn't need a timeline or a voice. It was understood.

Commercial flying at its finest. God, I missed the private planes. I was undeniably accustomed to that lifestyle. I could've flown with better accommodations but I wanted to maintain a low profile. Flying with the rest of the public gave me the willies. Public transportation always entailed crying babies and smelly people all jammed together like packaged sardines. An assortment of cheap department store cologne and stale air assaulted my nostrils, making my nose hairs twitch. My only saving grace was the fact that I got a window seat in the exit row for my long legs. I could put in my earbuds and lean my body against the window. I was a pretty intimidating guy. I was over six foot and built like a brick house. My jagged scar from the top of my eyebrow down to my jawline elevated fear levels. I wasn't vain in the least but I used my body to ward off potential people who wanted to chitchat, especially when it didn't involve an attractive woman. *If it weren't for a woman, then what was the point?* Hell, I had enough friends but there were never enough good-looking women to keep me warm at night.

I loved all types of women. Of course, I did have a special type. Curvy. Yep, that's it. I wanted a woman with meat on her bones. I didn't want to fuck a skeleton. All sharp planes poking into me? No, thank you. I wanted to be able to dig in to her fleshy sides as she rode me. The size of her breasts didn't matter as long as I had a handful; anything more than that and I risked spraining my tongue!

Thank God, the flight from New York to Indiana was a short one. By the time we debarked my legs had cramped and my head pounded as though it were a two-year-old crudely banging on pots and pans.

I navigated my way through the airport easy enough and was on the freeway toward the house that Forrest took upon himself to fix up. He had taken a drastic turn since moving to Lakeshore. I'm positive it had more to do with the woman he was head over heels for. I couldn't wait to meet the tail that had captured the once notorious bachelor. Although, if he was anything like his brother, once they fell, they fell hard, and never looked back. Simply thinking of settling down had my dick shrinking as though I had jumped into the freezing waters of the Pacific.

I got out of the car and looked up at the whimsical house. Had to hand it to him; when he did something, he went all in. It had to have cost him a pretty mint to fix up. It practically screamed money pit. I shook my head, picturing Forrest starring in the movie instead of Tom Hanks. I slung my bag over my shoulder and walked up the rickety porch, praying that he left the door open. Not that that would stop me; I'd find a way in regardless. Silly locks kept me out only long enough to pick them open. It simply made it hell of a lot easier to walk in then it did to break in. *Was it considered breaking and entering if*

I had been invited?

I twisted the brass knob and swung the door open. I stepped into the foyer, allowing my eyes to adjust to the darkness, and scanned the layout. *Damn, this place was massive.* Forrest and the crew he had hired made a decent dent on the interior. There were rooms upon rooms, with nooks and crannies all over the place. It suited Forrest well. He was built much the same way. Underneath all the hard shit he projected, he was a genuinely nice and loyal guy with a solid foundation. The type of guy you wanted in your corner when shit hit the proverbial fan.

Good thing I brought my bed in a bag. The floor in the dining room looked uncomfortable. More like a bed made from porcupine needles. My bed in a bag couldn't be construed as a thick mattress but I've slept on worse. From the sound of things, Forrest wanted this job done as quickly as possible. In return, I would suck it up. This wouldn't be an indefinite stay. Soon I would be back in my apartment and kicking my feet up in my recliner. I sighed with sentimental longing.

I set up my laptop on the bar in the kitchen and planted my ass on the hard stool. My back was ramrod straight as I dug into Eugene's life. This guy was a piece of work. He held no job, was abusive to his ex-old lady, and a drug addict. A real winning catch, if you ask me. The mugshot of him confirmed it: nothing but a greasy twat-bag. There was no charisma about him. His eyes were void of any emotion. Empty, hollow pits. This guy, no doubt about it, was dangerous but not enough that he couldn't be dealt with easily. Laying the groundwork before we went off half-cocked was essential.

Finding him proved to be easier than I had thought. Every city had a squatter house on the outskirts of town. I had mapped out my coordinates of each vacant house and its proximity to the ex's home. The logical choice would be the one closest so he could get to her quickly at any given moment. However, strung-out people don't always make logical choices. That's why I chose a couple of them and waited.

As darkness fell, I scooted out of my rental and gingerly strolled the short distance to the house. There had been no movement in the hour that I had sat canvassing it. Regardless, I needed to be able to peek inside to make sure that it was indeed empty. My feet moved with urgency the closer I got, using the cloak of night to cover me. The cover of darkness wasn't needed but, better safe than sorry. Broad daylight brought about questionable stares and potential witnesses. Addicts were unpredictable and I wanted the plan to go in our favor.

I slowed my steps as the side of the house came into view. Part of the siding was missing. The pink coloring of the insulation stuck out like a sore thumb. I kept low and out of sight as I walked around to the back of the home. The only sounds were of my boots hitting the yard laden with patches of weeds. The slight crunch was no louder than what an animal would conjure up. I wasn't being super quiet. My instinct told me that this house was clear. Not a soul had disturbed its slumber since it had been abandoned. I climbed the back steps to the door and twisted the knob. It was locked. I peered in the window and saw nothing but bareness. There was no garbage littered around or any sign that the guts of the home had been disturbed. I stuffed my hands into my pockets and walked back toward the rental. One down, two more to go.

I decided to take a chance on the house farthest from the ex's and the farthest from town. This one was a little trickier to get close to. I couldn't just walk up on it and pretend that I was in the neighborhood. It was on a back country road. I spotted an old trail or drive of some sort. Before I pulled in, I cut the headlights and then swung on to the dirt path and cut the engine. Rows of corn stalks on both sides provided the perfect cover. I pulled in deep enough to be completely camouflaged to any passerby. I looked at my watch and noted the coordinates. Not that there was a chance in hell I'd get lost. Try navigating through the desert that was as hot as the devil's ass crack without a fucking landmark anywhere. I left my vehicle and pulled on my leather gloves. I grabbed my bag and sifted through the small pocket until I located the two tracking devices. They were as slim as my thumbnail and no larger than a popcorn kernel: easy to hide and largely unnoticeable. They looked like a shorn piece of slate to the untrained eye.

I began the short trek to the house, if you could call it that. I stopped short of the edge of the corn row and took in my surroundings. The house sagged and looked as though it used all of its effort to stay on its foundation. The siding drooped and broke off in jagged pieces. Cocklebur and crabgrass had snuffed out the once smooth Kentucky bluegrass. A beat-up Chevy Cavalier sat in the front, parked crookedly on the frayed yard. The car didn't belong to Eugene––that I knew––but that didn't mean he didn't use it from time to time, if it actually still ran. I stealthily made my way to the back of the house with the darkness of night cloaking my movements. The moon knew my agenda and stayed hidden. Moving silently through the tall weeds, I barely made a sound.

The enclosed porch at the back provided plenty of cover.

As I neared the dilapidated house, I could hear the psychedelic tempest of "White Room" by Eric Clapton. *At least these guys had good taste in music.* I noticed a tattered sheet covering the windows on the side of the house. As I moved toward it, the music got louder. A soft glow peeked out from the sheet. I could easily see into the room without them noticing that I was there. Eugene and two other men lounged, stoned out of their minds, on a broken-down couch. The small camping lantern illuminated the room. They were so doped up that they appeared lifeless. A small twitch of the face or arm proved that they weren't. An old CD player sat in front of them, on a tipped over cardboard box. I leaned back and looked up at the second story. *No lights. Excellent.*

I snuck toward the back and shimmied my way up the back porch and onto the roof. I grinned as a door appeared, allowing an easy entrance. I crouched as I made my way over. I peeked through the grimy glass pane. It was a direct doorway into a bedroom. *Score! Fuck, this seemed way too fucking easy.* My gut wasn't screaming for me to become invisible and no sweat beaded anywhere along my skin. I marked this as go-the-fuck ahead and enter. I twisted the doorknob silently, moving it meticulously slow. The door groaned at the intrusion but not loud enough to disturb the party downstairs. The room was pitch-black and empty, my two favorite things for this type of work. I pulled a miniature flashlight from my cargo pocket and flicked it on. Simply enough light to get the job done and not alert anyone.

My boots swiftly covered the ground in the room. Clothes were strewn haphazardly. In the far corner sat a mattress that had seen better days. Hell, the no-tell-motel screamed five stars compared to this shit hole. I did a quick cursory glance around the room and spotted exactly what I needed. I sifted through a pair of disgusting pants to locate his wallet. I needed to make sure that this was his shit. *Bingo!* I slipped the wallet out and opened up the flap. Luck was on my side tonight. After I confirmed his ID, I inserted the first tracker into one of the empty credit card slots. I put the pants back on the floor and snatched one of his worn-out shoes. I lifted up the insole and deposited the second tracker. Once that was finished, I exited the same way that I had come in. I jumped down from the roof and strode back to the rental, giggling like a little schoolgirl on the inside.

I opened the door and glided the gear into neutral. I hung onto the steering wheel and backed the car onto the asphalt. I reversed my position and pushed the car far enough away and hopped in the driver seat. The engine purred to life. I powered the window all the way down and let the fresh air clear my mind. The adrenaline seeped from my pores and drifted out in to the night air.

MACK 2

BEFORE I CALLED IT A night, I synced the track-ers to my phone and laptop. *Looks like the douchebag hadn't moved.* Too bad. I really looked forward to catching the sleaze doing something so that I could slam my gorilla fists in his face. I would love to witness the look of fear radiating from his eyes. Put there from yours truly. He would get a fight that would render him six feet under. There was a perverse satisfaction from taking control from a person, especially when it came from a person who had no moral compass. Predators were all the same. They preyed on the weak to feed the monster within. Present to them someone of higher caliber and more vicious, and they folded like sniveling babies. Every predator talked a big game to their victims but when the tide rose, they sunk hastily, begging for their lives. Even trained assassins had a breaking point. There was nothing more I loved than finding exactly where that point was.

I heard the porch groan with the weight of a body. The creaks gave a better warning than the shrill of an alarm. There was no need to open my eyes because even in my deepest dream state they stayed open. I continued my even breathing, occasionally letting out a deep snore. The light of dawn cast brilliant gold lighting around the room. Once they finished the house, it would be stunning. My ears twitched, listening to the footfalls. Whoever was entering the house was practically silent. The only sound that registered his proximity was the light swish of clothing. Plenty of missions had honed my ability to pick up on the tiniest of nuances. The guy was big, probably around my height and build. *Hmm...* The anticipation of a challenge tossed a heavy dose of adrenaline and excitement into my veins. My heart rate accelerated, echoing loudly within the confines of my body. Out of my peripheral, the guy stood, staring at me. I could feel the weight of his thoughts as he ran through all of the options of how to dispose of me.

My limbs screamed at me to move, counter, and gain the advantage. Instead, I lay there pretending to sleep much like the possum. The intruder came closer, almost in my direct line of vision. His palm reached down preparing to cover my mouth and nose. *Fuck that bullshit. Not today.* With lightning quickness, I snatched his hand and bent it back farther than it was meant to go, applying pressure to render the guy immobile. Swiftly, I swung my leg up and around the guy's torso and flung him to the ground. I moved to straddle over him in order to start viciously pounding my fists when the fucker straight up donkey laughed. Clearing the red haze from my eyes, I looked at the target beneath me. *What the fuck!*

"You idiot. I could've killed you." I laughed back at him, never letting go of my hold.

Forrest kept right on laughing. "No you wouldn't, you big pussy."

I finally let go after another torturing moment because

I could. He sat up and rubbed his wrist, still laughing. He would be one hard motherfucker to obtain information from. He was one of those who would die before they broke. That's why I trusted him with my life.

"Please. I'm the pussy who had you in a pretty tight hold, ready to snap your wrist like a twig. So who is the pussy now?" I rubbed the sleep off my face, now acutely aware of my surroundings.

"You know I love pussy. Come here and give me some love." He wrestled me backward and slapped a big wet kiss on my forehead.

"You know you are one twisted fuck." I smacked him upside the head.

We both laughed as I climbed off him. We meandered into the kitchen. He grabbed a beer for us and we got down to business. Now was the best time to formulate a game plan and have it sealed airtight before it was put into motion.

"What's your girl say about what you are doing?"

He kept his head bent as he peered over the computer, not saying a word.

"Ah, she doesn't know." I whistled nonchalantly. "Probably better in the long run anyway."

"I bet my last dollar that she would be happy that he wouldn't bother her ever again. Just not thrilled about how it's going to go down. Something that she doesn't ever need to know about."

"Am I going to get to meet the infamous woman who managed to capture you?"

"Sure, why not? Not like you have a chance in hell of stealing her from me."

I squinted. "Challenge accepted, bro."

He chuckled. "All right, fucker, let's hash this out. I want this done in the next couple of days before he makes another move or runs."

"He won't. He is holed up in one of the abandoned houses on the edge of town. I paid the place a visit. He was high as a kite. Couldn't tell his head from his ass."

He looked up at me with deep frown lines. "What the fuck, man? You trying to blow it?"

"Sorry, man. I want to get this guy so bad that I'm not thinking straight."

"Exactly my point. You better check that caveman shit at the door if we are going to pull this off. We can't go off half-cocked. Damn it." He pinched his fingers along the ridge of his hairline. "We are a team."

I nodded, because what else was there to say? He was right. There was no sense letting my pride get in the way. We were both trained differently and had a multitude of strengths when combined. There was no doubt that he or I could pull this off alone but he asked for my help. That's what I was here for, not to go it alone. His phone buzzed and he got this stupid look on his face. God, it was disgusting to look at. It was all dopey and shit. I made gagging sounds as his fingers typed back a message. Of course he ignored me, not even choosing to acknowledge my prepubescent behavior.

"Speak of the devil. That must be your favorite tail." I tried to snatch the phone from his hands but he was quicker.

"Don't you ever speak about her like that ever again!" he ground out between his teeth.

I threw my hands up in surrender. "Stand down. I'm just playing." I chuckled inwardly.

Stupid fuck was so whipped. Don't get me wrong; I loved women––just not enough to want to settle down or get that glossy-eyed reading a text. I only wanted that look when I was balls deep inside a tight and warm center of a beautiful woman. Forrest grabbed the aerial shot of the rundown house that I had printed out. *Guess playtime was over.* While he studied it, I regurgitated the specifics of where Eugene laid his head. Getting in and out of the house would be a piece of cake. *Shit, I already proved that.*

"Forgot to mention that I put a tracker on him. I'll send you the link so that you can sync up your phone. I already synced mine. Our phones will ping when he is on the move. No more surprises for Candice. Between the two of us, we should be able to intercept him before he gets anywhere near her."

"Good job. That's a nice little token. I'm hoping that we will move in long before we have to rely on it."

The smile that lit his face was enough to scare seasoned men. If I hadn't known him personally his facial features right this moment looked downright psychotic. Forrest had a dark side to him that not many knew about. When you got on his bad side, look out—he would not hesitate to fuck you up in the most heinous ways. We hashed out more logistics and my cover story. This was beginning to be one of my favorite gigs. I got to snuff out a piece of shit and use my carpentry skills. *Hot damn!* I enjoyed restoring things to their former glory. I hardly ever got the chance anymore, usually going from one job to another with no downtime in between. Working alongside Forrest again was a bonus.

My ears perked at the sound of the front door opening. I stood on high alert. Forrest's laughter pierced through my zone and I relaxed.

"That's Sal and Enzo. Stand down, soldier." He cackled, as two men walked in the kitchen.

"Sal, Enzo, this is Mack. He is a good friend of mine and he has come down to help us out for a couple of days."

I shook hands with each of the men. They had good, firm handshakes without including any strong holds. Enzo seemed to be good-natured, with amusement surrounding him. He welcomed me with open arms, so to speak. I immediately liked him. He was one of the guys you'd go grab a beer with at the end of the day. Sal appeared to be more of a wary person. His eyes weren't cold but they held a healthy measure of curiosity and cautiousness. Couldn't blame him one bit. I would be, too, with an outsider entering my nicely controlled environment. He was another one I liked immensely. They both fit my personality to a tee. I would enjoy getting my hands dirty as I worked alongside these two.

"Nice to meet you guys. Looking forward to working with you." I smiled, while I finished up my assessment of them.

"You got any experience in construction or carpentry?" Sal questioned, remaining on edge.

"Well, let's see. Nope but I do dabble in restoration when I have down time. Will that get me a spot with the crew?" I said sarcastically.

Sal grumbled to himself and walked out of the room, knowing that he had been bested.

"Welcome. I could use the help. Sal has more than he needs." He slapped me on the back, chuckling. "Come on, let me show you what the overall game plan is and what I'm working on now."

"Sounds great." I rubbed my hands together, eager to start.

I started working in the grand room with the ornate fireplace. I stared at the ensemble and mesmerized every facet. In a matter of seconds, the fireplace came to life in my mind. Giddy with the geek in me, I ran out and snagged some of Enzo's tools and went right to work. I had found my groove about midway through the afternoon when a knock on the front door broke into my happy place. I ignored it and went back to stripping the old finish. *Fuck! Didn't anyone hear the door but me? I was not the fucking butler.*

The persistent knocking irritated my nerves. No one else appeared to jump up and get the door, so I guess it became my duty. I set my sander down, crossed through the foyer and swung open the door. My eyes rounded and a cocky grin spread outward from my lips. I may have licked them, who knew. *Damn. This chick was sexy as all hell.* Tall, blonde, and holding a couple of pizza boxes. My mouth watered from all three characteristics. I raised my hand and perched it along the doorframe, blocking her entry.

"Do you like what you see?" My voice was chock-full of lust.

The beauty openly laughed in my face.

Okay, maybe I was getting rusty. Nah, I only needed to change my game plan.

"Move, you big 'ol tease. I got hot pizza to deliver." She barreled right past me and headed right for Forrest.

That sucks. Can't be hitting on my buddy's woman. I would definitely do so—in a joking manner, of course. What fun would it be if I didn't harass him from time to time? I whistled on my way back to the kitchen, more jovial than ever. I grabbed a bunch of paper towels and loaded my plate with pizza that smelled delicious. I was hungrier than I had thought.

"Candice, this ugly brute is Mack. He is a good friend of mine," Forrest said between mouthfuls of pizza.

She shook my hand. "Nice to officially meet you. Thanks for helping me bring in the pizza," she taunted me.

A huge laugh escaped. "It was my pleasure. I think I like you, Candice."

"At least you're not hard on the eyes. Makes your personality easier to tolerate."

"Fuck, if you weren't Forrest's, I'd make you mine."

She playfully slapped my cheek. "Only in your dreams."

After the much-needed break, we all went our separate ways. I slipped my earbuds in and checked for the dull look from the commercial stripper that I had used. It had plenty of time to work. Indeed, the wood no longer looked glossy. I grabbed a dull scraper from the toolbox and began the tedious job of removing the old finish off the wood mantel. Whoever had originally designed this piece had exceptional talent. I had to admire their craftsmanship. One of these days, I'd be as talented in creating something so beautiful. I carefully ran the scraper along the grain so that I didn't gouge any of the wood. This was a delicate process. If I nicked the wood with too much pressure, it would be ruined. I loved this mind-numbing work. Everything else in my brain shut down. For a little while, the white noise in my head went silent.

My phone buzzed with an alert. I pulled it out of my pocket. *Shit!* That motherfucker was on the move. I set my tools down and sprinted to where Forrest was working. I hollered his name and held up my phone, trying to get his attention. The dumbass had his headphones on and couldn't hear shit. When I got close enough, I swatted the headphones from his head.

He staggered backward. "What the fuck?"

"I got a ping. We need to leave right fucking now." My brows furrowed into one as my anger grew to intense proportions from his stupidity.

The house was alive with a plethora of loud sounds. *You can't keep someone safe when you drown everything out.*

He knows this.

"Where is he headed?"

He knew damn well where that fucker was headed. I didn't need to throw it in his face an I-told-you-so. "Toward Candice's house."

We flew out of the house and to the car. Forrest peeled out and headed in what I assumed was the direction of her house. I could tell by the way that he gripped the steering wheel that she wasn't answering his calls. Adrenaline pumped viciously through my veins.

"She isn't answering. I'm hoping that she's at the apartment. Let's assume that she isn't and be ready for anything."

I smiled wickedly as I lifted up my pant leg. On the left inside of my ankle nestled a Ruger. "I won't use it unless I have to. We will stick to the plan."

He nodded his head in agreement. He stopped and killed the engine when he pulled in behind Candice's car. We simultaneously shut our doors as quietly as we could. If Eugene was in there, we didn't want to draw his attention to our presence. Better to have the element of surprise on our side. Forrest motioned with his hands for me to take the front and right rear of the house. He would take the opposite and we would meet in the back before we entered the house.

I silently crept alongside the house, occasionally peeking in a window. I saw nothing and heard nothing but my own intake of breath. I continued around the house until I met up with Forrest. He was on the toes of his boots, watching through the window. He moved to the side for me to take a look. Eugene had her cornered. Her body shook with fear.

"You think we should interrupt them?" I whispered, wanting to know how Forrest wanted to proceed.

"I think we give her a minute to decide if she is going to fight him."

I didn't think that was the best plan but this was his woman and his call. If she were mine, I would have already taken out the son-of-a-bitch and then asked questions later. My mind raced over all the potential ways to kill a man. I smiled sadistically at Forrest. He would know what I was thinking. Out of the corner of my eye, I caught Candice ramming her knee into his groin. The ear-piercing scream jostled us into action.

We barged into the back door and ran into the kitchen. Candice held the phone in her hand, talking to the 911 operator. We went over to Eugene as soon as Forrest made sure that Candice was okay. We picked him up off the floor by his armpits. We pushed him into the kitchen chair and stood guard so he wouldn't make a move. We glared at the son-of-a-bitch until a banging on the door told us that the police had arrived.

Candice let them in and they barreled into the kitchen as though they were cow wranglers. He sat, painfully subdued. We graciously moved out of their way. They wrenched his arms behind him and slapped on the hand-cuffs. They read him his rights as they hauled him up and out to their cruiser. Forrest and I took a seat in the kitchen and waited for them to come back inside and ask us a bunch of questions. Our shoulders shook with silent laughter, like two kids in the principal's office waiting for detention.

Candice stormed over to Forrest, madder than a wet hornet.

He grinned up at her as she towered over him. "You are kick ass, woman. I've never been so turned on in my entire life. I couldn't be more proud of you for taking him down."

Her anger dissipated at his compliment. "He deserved worse. Thank you for coming to my rescue. How did you even know I was here?"

He chanced a glance at me. "You didn't need to be rescued. You took care of business all by yourself. I tried calling you. When you didn't pick up, I got worried. I came straight here."

She tilted her head toward me. "And why are you here?"

I chuckled. "For backup. Looks like we got here a little too late. Although, I do have to agree with Forrest––that was fucking hot."

She laughed at me. "You better watch it. I have more where that came from. It might just have your name written all over it."

I winked at her. "I like my women feisty."

Forrest leaned over and smacked the back of my head.

One of the cops came back in and took our statements. He looked over at Candice. "My partner is taking him to the precinct. He will be arrested for violating the protective order. I can't say for sure if he will be charged or serve jail time."

She whipped her head around. "What? I showed you the restraining order. He clearly violated its no contact terms as well as threatened me." She threw her hands up in the air. "Does he have to physically hurt me or terminate my life before ya'll start taking this shit seriously?"

Forrest threw the car keys, which I easily caught in midair. Forrest had this shit handled. I didn't need to be around any longer. It wasn't really any of my business. Plus, he would clue me in when he came back to the house. I wanted to make a quick stop at the precinct. I knew one of the detectives and he owed me a favor. I had yet to cash in the favor he owed me from basic. I hadn't realized that he lived here until I had read some of the police reports. *Lucky for me that I had discovered that little nugget of information.*

I walked out of the precinct feeling damn proud of myself. Detective Matthews promised to let me know what was going on with Eugene. I didn't even have to call in my favor with him. Eugene had quite the reputation around here for getting into trouble. He had yet to be able to evade the law and with my help wouldn't see daylight ever again. He would be one less strain on the system. Unfortunately, another lowlife would take his place. The world was busting at the seams with them. My phone buzzed with an incoming text as I slid in the driver seat. I pulled my phone out and opened it up.

ANY INFO?

Forrest probably had a quick minute and needed to be reassured that Eugene hadn't been released.

YEAH. SAFE FOR THE TIME BEING. I'LL PICK YOU UP IN THE MORNING.

Only a teaser; right now, all he had to know was that for the night he wouldn't have to worry about watching over Candice. She was out of harm's way for the evening. With the edge taken off for the next few hours, I headed back to the house with visions of a deep and uninterrupted sleep looming in my future. Eugene would be released tomorrow. I had worked with Forrest enough to know the way that his mind worked. I hoped that son-of-a-bitch enjoyed his few remaining hours because I sure as hell would enjoy snuffing out the rest of them.

MACK 3

I WAITED FOR FORREST TO GET his lovesick ass out to the car. It was as though I were waiting on a chick to get ready. Took fucking forever. I understood he needed an extra minute. You never knew if you were going to come back from a mission or not. Best to cherish every moment than to regret any minute you wasted.

"Whistling that twisted song again?" I dryly commented. Whenever Forrest was in job mode, psyching himself up, he whistled "Twisted Nerve" by Bernard Herrmann. It crept me the fuck out.

"You know what kind of day it is then." He grinned.

"Sure do."

We rolled up to the Victorian. We made sure to maintain our presence here all day. Our alibi would be airtight but in case shit went wrong, then it was good to have potential witnesses, who could validate our alibi. Once Sal and Enzo and the rest of the crew showed up to work, we shut any talk of the mission down.

Stripping the wood down to its original material was equivalent to stripping down a woman. It took time, patience, and finesse. Underneath all the outer layers was where the natural beauty lay hidden. Rushing to the finish line always resulted in a poor outcome.

During lunch Forrest and I slinked upstairs for privacy,

making sure that our plan was airtight.

"Anything else that you can think of?" Forrest asked for the thousandth time.

"Nope. I think we have every plan possible in place. If shit gets hairy, we split up and meet back at the Victorian." I clapped a hand on his shoulder. "This will be one of our easiest marks. Don't worry so much. Piece of cake, brother." I smiled with the hopes of reassuring his doubts.

The both of us were well-oiled machines. Once we had set our sights on our targets, it was hard to disengage. Forrest was overly cautious because it was personal for him. When you took out your feelings, making yourself dead inside, any lingering doubts disintegrated.

We joined the others before too long and swiftly integrated back in with the crew. They were an easygoing bunch. They worked hard but didn't let it consume them. The house was shaping up quicker than I would have imagined. My leave from Lakeshore was fast approaching. I had mixed feelings about returning to an empty apartment, awaiting orders on the next job. I didn't dwell on it too long. My hands fell into a steady groove, allowing my mind to peacefully go blank.

Darkness settled around us. The crew packed up and headed to parts unknown. Once the house became silent, we loaded up our bag and tossed it in the trunk of the car. We drove to the Hickey to drum up another piece of our alibi. The bar had a small-town quality to it. It wasn't pretentious and catered to the drinking crowd. Everyone was welcomed. Forrest saddled up to the bar and I hit the head.

I made my way to the bar but stopped dead in my tracks as I got a good look at the bartender. Not only did my body stand erect, my dick instantly became rock hard. I shifted Jr. and walked calmly to the barstool. *What the fuck?* What was I——fourteen again, copping my first feel of a pair of tits? *Jesus, Mack, get a hold of yourself.* My tongue darted out, wetting my lips, as she strolled over to me.

"What's your poison, sugar?"

You: naked, and moaning my name as I slam into your drenched pussy. "Bourbon, neat."

She nodded her head and walked toward the liquor bottles stacked along the far end of the bar.

I twisted the barstool toward Forrest. "Who is that and where the hell have you been hiding her?"

He laughed. Then took a healthy swig of his beer. "Don't know her. I'm sure if you ask Candice, she would know. Or hell, here is a brilliant idea. Why don't you ask the lady herself?"

"Dick! Not sure why I hadn't thought of that. Fucker," I smarted back.

The voluptuous redhead placed my drink in front of me. "You want me to start a tab?"

"Nope." *Brilliant——exactly the smooth conversation I wanted.*

"That'll be ten dollars, sugar." She winked.

My dick noticed and poked his head up, trying to get a good look at the gorgeous woman before me. I pulled a twenty out of my wallet and handed it to her. When she went to grab it, I held onto it, not letting her take the money yet. "What's your name? Or shall I call you Ruby?"

Her lips curved up at the corners. "Abbie."

I let go. The money slipped through my fingers as she pulled it away and walked to the register. I ogled her backside, committing it to memory. She was curvy in all of the right places, enough for my large hands to grab onto. Damn, if her eyes weren't the darkest shades of green I had ever seen. They were as dark as the pine needles of the Sitka spruce along the Oregon coast. I'd bet money that she was as unique as the evergreen itself. She would be worth staying awhile longer for.

Forrest elbowed me in the ribs. "What?" I barked, pissed at him for ruining my visions of Abbie.

"Time to roll." He snorted.

I looked at my watch to confirm that we had been here longer than I had realized. *Shit!* We had been sitting here for over two hours. My drink was barely touched and the horrendous karaoke in the background never registered until I got up from the barstool. I had spent the entire time fixated on my favorite bartender, who pointedly ignored me the whole time.

We furtively left the tavern and headed out to the middle-of-nowhere drug house. An overgrown tractor entrance surrounded by thick cornstalks provided all of the camouflage we needed. I covered my hands with thin leather gloves. I snatched my night-vision goggles and set out through the field, covering Forrest's back. We stealthily made our way through the maze of corn; not a sound could be heard. We were sheathed within the evening's cloak. We both bent at the knee about a hundred yards from the rundown house. We took off our night-vision goggles and allowed our eyes to adjust to the blackness.

Candles flickered inside and illuminated the place in an eerie glow. Shadows danced along the tattered sheers. We counted possibly five people in the dilapidated house. We waited until the house grew quiet and the candles burned out.

Forrest and I nodded to each other. We replaced our goggles. I took off the bag and snatched only what we needed. With our pockets full, we crept to the house. The second story had a sagging porch attached. The room located beyond that door was where I had found Eugene the last time.

I bent down on one knee so that Forrest could use my leg to boost himself up. This was the quickest way for the both of us to shimmy our way onto the roof. He lay on his stomach and reached his hand over the porch toward me. I felt his hand close over mine. Inch by slow inch, he pulled me up next to him. We pushed into a sitting position and listened for any kind of footfalls or voices. Hearing absolutely nothing, we slunk toward the door. Forrest twisted the handle of the door. My body went rigid and I held my breath, anticipating the creak of the door. It gave without much force. The door swayed open without so much as a groan. I slowly let out the breath that I had been holding. Adrenaline pumped through my veins, making my heart beat in rapid succession.

The room remained void of any homey furnishings. The stained mattress lay in the exact same corner. A ripe, pungent stench permeated the room. A naked torso lay sprawled upon the bed. We slunk along the wall and crept closer. Eugene lay passed out in all of his scrawny, emaciated glory. Track marks decorated his body. Dark shadows perched along his lifeless skin. Forrest swiftly positioned his body on top of Eugene. I held his arms and legs securely, incapacitating him. Eugene had lapsed into some drug-induced high, barely flinching when Forrest held him down.

I grabbed the needle full of heroin and carefully handed it to him. He seized the needle with his gloved fingers and jammed it into Eugene's neck. He pushed the plunger of the syringe and emptied the contents straight into his jugular vein. My ears were perked and attuned to the slightest of sounds. I had to be vigilant so that Forrest could work without any interruptions. Forrest secured him until his lips turned a cold blue. He pushed his body off and stood next to me as Eugene's body convulsed with muscle spasms. His body tensed and seized. We watched as the last breath of life passed through him. The atmosphere grew still.

Forrest nodded to me, signaling that there was no longer a pulse. We had extinguished Eugene's life in a matter of minutes. I felt nothing as I looked over at the scumbag. The job was done. Forrest set up the scene with finesse. Once everything was completed, we retraced our steps out of the house and back to the edge of the field.

I took the bag of items that needed to disposed of. All of the incriminating evidence would be two states away in some landfill. We settled back in the kitchen of the house, unwinding with a couple of beers. I clinked mine with Forrest's and then chugged it back.

He squeezed my shoulder as a thank-you for putting my life on the line for him. "See you in the morning."

"Yep. I'm sleeping in, so don't come calling bright and early."

"Well deserved, my friend."

I hadn't done shit. I would have loved to be the one to jam that needle in the prick's neck but I'd agreed to tag along. Forrest had to be the one to kill. This way, he controlled the entire outcome and witnessed the fucker take his last breath.

I settled on my makeshift bed, resting my hands under my head, thinking about my little Ruby back at the bar. Her thick, pouty mouth drove me wild. Thinking about her curves had my dick saluting. *Fuck!* I needed to get laid. *Screw it.* I threw the covers over my face and shut my eyes. The silence surrounding me finally lulled me to sleep even though my blood zinged in my veins.

I groaned when my knees hit the floor as I rolled clumsily out of bed. I was half tempted to slump back to the floor. I picked my old ass up off the hardwood, wincing as my long healed war wounds flared to life. Mortality sucked. I wanted to go back in time to when I felt invincible. I stood in Forrest's kitchen, making a pot of coffee, and contemplated my next move. The house would be done soon. I wasn't eager to get back to my old life: an empty apartment and endless jobs that amounted to absolutely nothing in the grand scheme of things. I had enough money to contemplate a career change. I lived frugally most of the time, anyway. My bank statements proved that. Almost every dollar I had made was tucked safely in its nest, waiting for me to spend it. Might be a good change to become partners with Forrest. The more time I spent here, the more I could envision myself setting down roots.

I let the music drown out my thoughts as I went to finish up the mantel. Pride welled in my chest as the mantel began to show signs of its new life. I admired my handiwork; a strong hand squeezed my shoulder. I twisted to my left, primed with the likeness of a death adder snake poised to strike. I loved these snakes. They could move from strike position, to envenoming, and then back to strike pose all within a fifteenth of a second. Their prey never saw their impending death.

I encountered Enzo's beaming face.

"Amazing job. I couldn't have done better myself. If you want a job, let me know. You are as good as hired."

"Thanks, Enzo. Not sure if I will be sticking around permanently or not. If I do and don't take Forrest's offer, then I will definitely hit you up."

"Whatever you want to do, kid, but you've got talent

that would be a shame to be wasted." He slapped my back and turned to walk out.

"I might be persuaded to help with certain projects if I do stay." My words caught his retreating back.

"Sounds like an arrangement that I can manage," he threw over his shoulder.

I shook my head at the craziness of it all. *What the hell was this place?* Maybe I was in the Bermuda Triangle. Maybe it was the farming and good 'ol boy mentality that made this town appear to be the set of Mayberry. I walked through the foyer on my way to greet the rest of the guys when Candice ran smack into my side with an *oomph* passing through her lips.

My hands braced her firm upper arms to steady her. "Where's the fire, little lady?"

Her eyes widened as she laughed like a lunatic. "Move, you big lug. Where is my man?"

I let go of her, stepped to the side, and pointed up the stairs. I wasn't going to get in her way. She looked as though she were on a mission. Far be it for me to step in her way and halt her forward momentum.

ABBIE 4

I BLEW AT THE STUBBORN STRANDS of fine hairs stuck to my perspiring face as I finished mopping the floors. I drew my shoulders back as I straightened, trying to loosen my tight muscles. I loved owning the bar. I had some incredible regulars who made putting up with the college crowd worth it. Tonight had been extra brutal. All night, the bar had been filled to capacity with people and the ka-ching of the till had sang its sweet melody. Nights like tonight kept the bar afloat during the slow months when the college crowd went home on break. I owned the entire building, so the only overhead cost was the liquor and a couple of employees. I wasn't complaining but my back sure as hell was.

The Hickey had been handed down to me from my father. I had grown up playing on the scuffed hardwood floors. Once I was old enough, I was behind the bar, slinging drinks, and I had loved every minute of it. I still did on most days. Every inch of this place was my home. Before my father had passed away, he signed the bar over to me. It had been a bittersweet deal. I could close my eyes and picture my father standing tall behind the bar, with a towel thrown over his shoulder and his head thrown back laughing at something Mr. Daniels had said. That old coot was as perverted as they came.

I never regretted my decision to stay and help my father run the bar. College life was not for me. I never had the ambition to obtain my degree. From the beginning, all I had wanted was to own this bar. I would have rather run it alongside my father but it hadn't been in the cards. Every year, the pain of losing him lessened as the memories of him stayed crisp in my mind. Some nights, when the place only had a few regulars, I could sense his presence. Every once in a while the scent of his Paul Sebastian aftershave would drift around me. That in of itself was comforting enough to know that I had made the right call to stay in my hometown and take over. Even if I had left to go to college, I knew in my heart that I would have come back. This place had embedded itself in my bones.

Moving slower than normal, I hit the lights, and made my way up the back stairs to my apartment. I entered the dark space. There was no need to turn on the lights. I had lived here for my entire life. I knew every inch of this place. The same furniture that I had grown up with sat in the exact spot. After my father had passed, I couldn't bear to move any of the pieces and make it my own yet. One day, I'm sure that I will but for now I felt content to be surrounded in its familiarity.

I climbed into my childhood bed and settled under the same comforter that I had as a little girl: sky-blue with daisies. I lay on my back, completely exhausted and yet unable to fall asleep. I stared up at the yellow ceiling paint. An image of a bad boy with a jagged scar played through my mind. He was the epitome of badass. His sculpted muscles stretched his already form-fitted shirt. His large frame had the ability to suck any available oxygen left in the room. His steel-gray eyes tore at my soul. An undercurrent of desolation surfaced long enough for me to see through his facade. Curiosity burned bright as I wondered what his story was.

The other guy he was with was Phoenix's brother. He had started dating Candice not too long ago. I had never met him but he had enough likeness to Phoenix to know that they were related. Phoenix and Lucy had recently wed and it had blown us all away. We had all figured that she would have married her long-time friend Gage. It's a small town where everyone knew your business, whether you wanted him or her to or not.

I gave the seductive stranger my name but hadn't learned his. I bet my girl, Marie, would know exactly who he was. You thought bartenders got the most up-to-date gossip. Nope. Hairdressers were the ones to obtain the juiciest chatter around. Total strangers spilled their guts while sitting in the chair.

Marie and I had been best friends since before we could talk. Joined at the hip was what most people said about us. That bitch left me a couple of years ago to go pursue her career in some swanky city in New York. I knew exactly where she went but I never gave her the satisfaction of acknowledging that part of her life. It had become a long-standing joke between us.

I had felt lost when she left, especially after my father died. It had become difficult to breathe some days with her so far away and my father gone for good. I was happy for her but even more elated that she had come home. We had chatted often but the calls could never replace her presence. My eyelids drooped while I mentally made a note to call her tomorrow and get the scoop.

MACK 5

I QUICKLY READ THE INCOMING TEXT from For-rest. That piece of shit, Eugene, was given a proper burial. As long as there was a burial, Forrest and I should not be under any suspicion. It's not as if Candice would want another autopsy done. She was probably more elated than we were that he was dead. Not that he deserved a burial but Riley needed to have closure. I'm sure as the years progress, she will forgotten him altogether. At least, that is my hope for her. I had to admit they made a pretty neat family. He had asked me to think about working with him but I wasn't entirely sure I wanted to reside permanently in Indiana.

As I reclined in the buttery leather of the private plane seat, the allure of being closer to friends gnawed at me as the jet headed closer to home. The job was finished. I either went back to my shitty apartment for good or took Forrest up on his offer. This last kill hadn't given me nearly the same satisfaction as it normally would have. Don't get me wrong; I still enjoyed the thrill of putting a hole in that motherfucker's skull. The difference this time was the lack of excitement of immediately procur-ing another assignment. Normally I'd skip into the boss's office to ask for my next job. My desire at the moment was to put my size-thirteen field boot up his ass.

Shortly after Eugene's overdose, I hit the tarmac and headed home. The first thing I did was to call my boss. I allowed my body to relax once we were airborne and the desert sand faded. I let my eyelids close and sank deeper into the chair. Visions of a fiery, redheaded Ruby floated through my mind. My favorite bartender might be the excuse I needed to go back for a bit. It would give me a chance to talk to Forrest about his offer. A smile tugged at the corners of my mouth the more I thought about it.

I snatched and twisted the wrist touching my shoulder. The painful whimper of the stewardess sliced through my kill-or-be-killed brain. I instantly let go. My eyes flashed open and zeroed in on the petite female I had nearly sent to the hospital with a broken wrist.

"I'm sorry if I hurt you," I said gruffly.

"It's okay. A little sore but nothing a little aspirin can't take care of. I should have known better than to put my hand on you while you were sleeping." She rubbed her wrist tenderly.

I winced. Hurting women was not something that I would ever tolerate. I've seen her on previous flights. She knew the dangerous kind of men who flew on this plane. Yet, I felt shitty about hurting her. To most people, her hand represented a simple gesture done every day. For me, it was automatically perceived as a threat. When I am awake, it's a totally different story. I have all of my senses functioning at a hundred percent and can tell the difference.

"I really am sorry. If there is a way that I can make it up to you––you be sure to let me know." I winked and flashed my most charming smile.

"We are landing soon," she replied coldly.

"Thank you."

She nodded and walked back to the front of the plane.

Somewhere along the line I'd lost my touch. Then again, I had just propositioned her and she was not that type of woman. She never utilized the mile-high card that I know of, and trust me—word gets around fast in our small circle. Not that I could even fit in that fucking hole because that was what it was: a hole. A man of my size needed space to properly fuck one of God's greatest treasures. I sure as hell loved to please them until they screamed his name.

I strode into my apartment, bypassed my chair, and haphazardly threw together a bag. I headed straight to my truck and hightailed it to the Midwest. I enjoyed the drive. The dark, empty roads made me feel as though I were the only soul around. Granited, it was well into the night and those not on the roads were sound asleep. I let the warm summer breeze float in the window as I hung my elbow out the window. By the time I pulled into the drive of Forrest's house, it was already midmorning. They should be up and eating breakfast by now.

I traipsed up the sturdy steps, pounded on the door, and then let myself in.

"Hope you made enough for me. I'm starving," I hollered through the open foyer.

"Unci Mack, Unci Mack. You come see me!" Riley squealed as she slammed into my legs.

I grabbed hold of her and tossed her into the air. Her giggles echoed through the foyer, making me feel lighter.

"You betcha, squirt. I missed my favorite girl." I gave her a smacking kiss on her pudgy cheek.

She nestled deeper into my neck. "You my favowite

guy."

Really! Could this kiddo get any cuter? There wasn't a single person she hadn't wrapped around her little finger, me included. Her lisp and huge heart were her charm. Her almond-shaped eyes didn't help either. They were almost too large for her petite face. Somehow it all worked. When she grew older, she would be the spitting image of her mother. Forrest better have a strong hold on her. The boys would be kicking down the door to date her. I had a good feeling that he would shoot first and then ask questions. I know that's exactly what I would do if I had a daughter. No boy or man would ever be good enough.

I strode through the house to the kitchen as though I belonged. My little squirt clung tightly around my neck.

Candice walked around the island and placed a gentle kiss on my cheek. "Good to see you. Are you hungry?"

"Starving. Are you going to share those delicious-looking pancakes?"

"Mommy made extwas. She aweways does, just in case you come by." Riley shimmied down and ran to her own chair.

"Ah, shucks. Thanks, Mom." I winked.

"Zip it and go grab your plate."

Her cheeks heated from Riley's slip of the tongue. My heart lightened further. There wasn't a soul in my life who had thought enough about me to be so endearing. The truth of her admission caught me off guard.

"You here for good?" Forrest slapped me on the back as he sauntered into the kitchen.

I shrugged. "Not sure yet. I'm taking it one day at a time."

He smirked. "Good enough for now."

We all loaded our plates and dug in.

Forrest wiped his mouth. "I'm heading to the office." He kissed the top of Riley's head. "Be good for your momma."

She rolled her eyes. "I aweways am Daddy. Duh."

He chuckled under his breath and then grabbed his wife heatedly. Shit, I could feel it from over here. After he kissed the hell out of her, he turned toward me. "You coming?"

"In a bit. I've got some things to take care of first."

"See you later then."

I finished scarfing down the pancakes as though I hadn't eaten for a week. Damn, they were really good. I got up and rinsed my plate before I set it in the sink.

I turned back around. "You need me to do anything before I head out?"

"Not a thing. Will you be back for dinner and how long are you staying?"

Candice's questions held no bite. She wasn't the type to get bent out of shape from my impromptu visit. She'd probably let me move in if I asked. I wouldn't take advantage of her hospitality.

"Only a couple of days, tops. If that is okay with you?"

"You know you are always welcome here. I've told you that a million times. I'll save a plate for you in case you don't make it in time for dinner."

I walked over to where she sat and kissed the top of her head. "Thanks."

"What about my kiss? I'm the favowite one."

I couldn't help but chuckle. "You are absolutely my favorite. I was only saving the best for last." I kissed her plump cheek as she beamed at her mother. "See you later."

They called out bye in unison.

I left the house and drove toward the apartment complex that Forrest used to live in. I was hoping that they would have a vacancy. I enjoyed staying with Forrest and his family but I also knew what it felt like to have guests overstay their welcome. Renting an apartment seemed like a logical next step. This way I wasn't locked into anything for a long period of time. It was the most logical decision at the moment.

I walked out of the office with a signed lease and the key in my hand. I'd have my stuff packed and shipped to this apartment. I'd only have to mooch off Forrest and his family for another week. I shouldn't think of Candice and Riley as his family. Truth be told, they were my family too. I was secretly thrilled that Riley called me Uncle Mack. I wouldn't have it any other way. When I first told Forrest that I would help him, I thought it would be an in-and-out job, with no strings attached. I would come back home and forget all about them until he or I called in a favor. The two of them had grown on me. They had entwined themselves around my heart. It was hard to believe for a cold-blooded killer with minimal morals.

ABBIE 6

"HEY, GIRL. WHAT ARE YOU up to?" I asked as soon as Marie had picked up.

"Nada. Just watching my niece prance around my living room in her underwear and a tiara."

"No way."

"Seriously. This girl cracks me up. The best free entertainment ever."

"I bet. She is a cutie. Takes after her aunt in the diva department.""Whatever. She made me paint her toenails this morning but she wouldn't let me paint them unless she took her clothes off first. We went around and around until I gave in. We compromised and kept her underwear on. I had to bribe her with candy just so she would put her clothes back on before my sister picked her up."

I laughed so hard that I got a stitch in my side. "Oh, I can believe that. Are you watching her until Gina gets out of work?"

"Yeah. She dropped her off this morning. Brandon got called into work so I told her to bring her by."

"What do you say we get some dinner after Gina comes and before I have to open?"

"Sounds like a plan. I'll meet you at Dispenza's around five."

"All right, girl. See you later."

"Bye."

I tied my hair into a messy bun, jacked up the volume of my Bluetooth speaker, and cleaned the apartment. I was the only one living in this small space and yet I managed to create a mess equivalent to a five-person household. Dirty dishes sat in the sink, last night's clothes were strewn across the chair in the living room, and dust bunnies partied on the scratched-up hardwood floor. *When had I found it acceptable to keep my home this messy?* About the time I spent most of my hours downstairs running the bar.

My bar wasn't specific to any genre of music. The jukebox held just about everything you could think of. Hits from Merle Haggard to Cypress Hill and everything in between; you never know what one of the customers would play. The same went for the local bands. There was no specific band that played. Anyone and everyone could play on the stage as long as they booked the slot and were legit. Hell, one night I had a polka band. That Saturday night, the bar was hopping with the biggest older crowd I have ever seen in my life. There was nothing better than watching a bunch of inebriated senior citizens dancing to the polka music. That night reminded me of my dad. I could envision him busting out his accordion and playing on the stage with them.

I lounged on the couch for a while before I had to meet up with Marie. I got sucked into watching a show on tiny houses. These people were transitioning from large homes to homes with less than one thousand square feet. Every episode, there would be a person who wanted large storage areas, larger bathrooms, and fully furnished kitchens. I was getting annoyed and even started yelling at the TV at the absurdity of it all. Yet, I couldn't make myself change the channel. Before I knew it, the day had flown by and I had to go meet my girl. It had been a couple of weeks since we had hung out. I was looking forward to catching up with her.

Dispenza's had the most amazing pizza. Nothing compared to Roselva's pies. I'm not sure where she picked up the recipe. All I knew was that every slice tasted like magic. Roselva was a trip. She was boisterous and unpredictable. Visiting her restaurant was like diving into a soap opera. The characters were the same but the drama was always entertaining and new. The place was unscripted. Roselva was the main attraction and she knew everybody's business. She said and did what she wanted. If you didn't like it, she'd kick you out and not be sorry about it.

I said a quick hello to Tracy, the waitress, and slid in the booth across from my best friend.

"Did you manage to get Lia to put her clothes on before your sister picked her up?"

"Girl, she threw a tantrum that I have never witnessed in my life. It became a battle of wills that I could not let her win. I managed to get her clothed right before Gina walked through the door. Then you know what she told my sister?"

"I have no idea but I bet it's a good one."

"She said, "Ant Mare is an asshole. She made me put my clothes back on.' I was torn between angry and bursting out in laughter. I know she heard that from her father because I don't swear in front of her and neither does her mom." She grabbed my arm. "I had to bite my lip so I wouldn't laugh as Gina scolded her for her language and then made her apologize to me."

I busted out laughing so hard that I spit out the Diet Coke that Marie had already ordered for me. "That is hilarious. Lia is only three. Where does she come up with this stuff?"

"I'm telling you, her father has a trucker's mouth and Lia picks up on everything. She is too smart for her own good."

"Gina has got her hands full, that is for sure."

"You ain't kidding. I love my niece but she is a walking advertisement for abstinence."

"Gina is a saint."

Tracy brought out our pizza and I dove in as though I hadn't eaten in days. I savored the first bite. When the garlic and oregano hit my taste buds, my eyes rolled upward, and I actually moaned out loud.

"This isn't a soft-porn flick, Abbie! It's a family restaurant. Keep your shenanigans at home, young lady," Roselva shouted from the kitchen through the cutout in the wall.

I covered my mouth and mumbled an apology, utterly embarrassed. That woman had the hearing capabilities of a pigeon. There was no way that my moan could have been heard two tables away, let alone thirty feet. I scanned the almost empty restaurant to make sure there weren't any small, impressionable children. Thankfully there wasn't.

I turned my attention back to Marie. She was practically doubled over, hysterically laughing.

"This is not funny. You wait until she turns her attention toward you. It won't be so comical then."

She laughed harder until soft snorts escaped. When I heard her snorting, I let loose my own chuckling.

"I don't know what's funnier: Roselva's comment or Lia's antics. Either way, this has been the best day ever!"

"Oh, shut up and eat. I've got to get to work soon." I tried out my most threatening glare, which only made her laugh harder.

I picked up my pizza and stuffed my mouth, making sure not to let another contented moan slip through. Marie's laughter finally subsided enough to eat. Every now and then, she would let out a little chuckle. God, I loved this woman. She was good for my soul.

"Have you seen that sexy-as-sin guy? He hangs out with Forrest," she blurted between mouthfuls.

"The one with the scar?"

"Yep. That's the one. Looks like he could make you cum a hundred different ways without even touching you."

"He came into the bar with Forrest awhile back. Didn't say much the whole time they were there. Do you know who he is?"

"Girl, you know I do. His name is Mack. I styled Candice's hair for her wedding. I paid extra attention when they talked about him. I couldn't figure out what he did for a living but from what I gathered, he is a straight-up badass. Forrest asked him to be his partner and Candice is hoping that he takes him up on it. She had said that her little girl had started calling him Uncle. She didn't want to see her daughter lose Mack this close to having already lost her daddy. Not that they were close but the burial was still fresh in her mind. She said that Riley needed all the strong male role models she could get. She also said that under the tough exterior, he was a big 'ol teddy bear."

"Wow, that's a lot of information. I can't believe you got all that in one sitting."

"Please——she was in my chair for an hour and Lucy went next. So they sat next to each other and gossiped the whole time. I smiled and only chimed in when they directed a comment my way. I play like I'm not even paying attention to the conversation. I'm practically invisible and that, my dear friend, is how I get all the juicy gossip."

I really was shocked that the two of them were that candid. Lucy and Candice were relatively private people. They didn't gossip about others and their lives. They were pretty hush--hush. They must have been extremely preoccupied to let their guard down like that. We all knew each other but Marie and I didn't run in the same social circle as Candice and Lucy. They mainly stuck to themselves but every now and then I would see Rebecca out with them. Rebecca would fit in their little group. She wasn't one to spread any rumors or jump on the gossip train. She worked for Phoenix, so it made sense that they would end up being friends. Plus, she rented Lucy's old house.

When Gage came in town, I would see him and Lucy at the bar. The bar used to be one of Lucy and Gage's favorite hangouts. That's where I had met him. Gage was one of the best lovers I've ever had. Of course, I would never in a million years tell him that. We would never have made it as a couple. I simply enjoyed using him for my pleasure and vice versa. He sure knew how to please a woman--multiple times a night. I shivered just thinking about it. It had been awhile since I've taken anyone home for the evening. *Mental note: find a suitable one-night stand.*

I swallowed the last bite of my pizza. "You coming in tonight for a drink?"

"I wish. I got a huge bridal party tomorrow, starting at nine in the morning. I don't want to be hungover for that." She rolled her eyes.

"Alrighty, girl." I looked down at my watch. "I've got to open."

We slid out of the booth and headed to the cash register.

"Call me tomorrow." I hugged her good-bye.

"You got it."

I plugged in the jukebox, walked over, and flipped the switch for the Open sign. The neon light hissed to life, signaling that the bar was open for business. Most of the other bars in town opened earlier in the day. I didn't open until later in the evening. My dad had told me that owning a bar wasn't all there was to life. If someone wanted a drink before seven then they could go to one of the other establishments. When he passed, I kept the same hours. This gave me most of the morning to sleep in and still have plenty of time to do what I needed before I opened. For not being open earlier, in the day I don't feel as though I lost that much of a profit to warrant changing the hours.

As soon as I stepped behind the bar, Mr. Daniels stepped through the doors. He slowly inched his way to the same barstool he always sat at. It was the one at the edge of the bar closest to the bathroom. I pulled out a glass to pour his favorite beer––Bud Light on tap. I set the glass on a napkin right in front of him.

"How's it going, Mr. Daniels?"

"It's better now that I got to see you," he said smoothly.

"You're such a charmer." I winked at him.

"You know it, young lady. I'd probably throw a hip out." His raspy laugh ended in a coughing fit.

"How's Mrs. Daniels doing?" I asked to change the subject.

"Old and crotchety. Always complaining that I spend too much time here. I wouldn't if she would quit nagging all the time."

The scowl on his paper-thin face was priceless. He looked more like a chastised little boy sulking. I know he loved his wife. They had been married for fifty-plus years. They never had any children, which I thought was a shame. Mrs. Daniels was the stay-at-home type. Best baker in town. Her snickerdoodle cookies were to die for. Every year for my birthday she would make me a dozen and send them in with Mr. Daniels. I would hide them until I went upstairs. I wasn't ashamed to admit that I sat in front of the TV and ate every damn one.

"Holler if you need anything," I told him as I went to serve the few customers who had walked in.

I walked over to the group of college kids who filled one of the round tables. "What can I get you guys?"

"Your phone number."

"It's what can I get you or get the fuck out," I spat.

"Feisty. I like that in my women."

I turned to head back to the bar when one of the jerks grabbed my hand. I whipped around and glared. He immediately let go.

"I'm sorry. Don't mind Jim—he is an asshole. We will start with a bucket of Coors."

My eyes hardened further, wanting to say something crude. Instead, I plastered a smile on my face and nodded. Sometimes, I really hated college boys. Other times, they were awesome to take home. They didn't want anything other than a good time. Mr. Hand Grabber was pretty cute. I could overlook his rude friend as long as they didn't make any more waves.

I set the bucket in the middle of the table. "You guys want to start a tab or pay as you go?"

Mr. Hand Grabber said, "We will pay as we go. Thank you."

I collected the money and went back to check on Mr. Daniels.

"You doing all right or do you want a fresh one?"

"I'm good right now. You okay? I saw one of those prissy boys grab your hand. You want me to go over there and kick his ass?"

I laughed and my mood brightened immediately. "Not yet. I'll let you know when I need you to teach them a lesson on respect."

He nodded as though what I had said was perfectly normal. He couldn't whip a dead snake without being sent to the hospital. It felt good to know that he cared enough to want to come to my aid. I could have kissed his cheek but I wasn't sure how strong his heart was.

"Let's go. This place is dead."

I heard the jerk shout from across the bar to his buddies who had went over to play pool. *Good. I hope you get the fuck out. You aren't welcome in my establishment.* He was good- looking in a pretty boy way. From the bottom of his expensive boat shoes to the top of his expertly styled cut, he screamed spoiled rich kid. I hated that type. They all had an air of entitlement that surrounded them. I guess money talked in their circles. In mine, flashing it around only made you an asshole. This town was down-to-earth. We didn't give a shit if you drove a beat-up, rusted-out piece of junk or a souped-up jaguar. We were all the same and demanded equal respect. That was the bottom line.

Once they headed out, I relaxed more. I hadn't real-ized how on edge I had been until they had left. The rest of the night sailed on with ease. The bar never exceeded its maximum occupancy but it did pick up later into the night.

I hit the switch for the lights multiple times in succession and called out, "Last call."

A chuckle escaped as the diehard customers scrambled for one last drink.

"I'll take a Bud Light."

I glanced up, recognizing the male voice from earlier.

"Sure thing." I popped the top off and handed him the beer.

Our fingers overlapped. I went to pull away but he held fast. "I wanted to apologize for my friend. He was being an asshole. Not all of us are like him and thank you for being cool about what he had said."

He let go of my hand.

"No need for you to apologize. It wasn't your remarks. For future reference, I wouldn't go around telling people that he is your friend. From what I could tell in the limited time that I spent in his presence, he only thinks of himself, and you will not even be a thought if ya'll get into trouble."

"Duly noted. I'm Travis, by the way."

"Abbie. Nice to meet you."

He looked down at his hand as though he were gathering courage. For what, I didn't know. I held my breath, waiting to see whether he would clue me in. When he finally looked up, I could clearly see the determination set in his gaze.

"Could I get your number? Maybe we could catch a movie and dinner one night this week."

"Or you could hang around until I closed and we can skip all this polite bullshit." I winked and stepped down the bar.

He was a looker with his blond cropped hair and sharp jawline. I was looking for a one-night stand and he would do nicely. I know he attended the university in town due to his slight Southern accent. He was in his early twenties. I hoped with the same stamina. It had been awhile and I was going to use him up.

Much to my surprise, Travis helped me with the closing duties. He mopped the floor as I cleaned the glasses and closed the register. He put away the mop and I locked up. There was something hot about watching a man in tight jeans wielding a cleaning utensil. I had a clear view of him stepping out of the storage room. He walked toward me with more confidence than when he had asked me for my number. *Yep, I was a sure thing.* There was no guesswork about what I wanted.

I seductively took my time walking across the floor. "Follow me."

I placed my greedy hand upon his taut chest, sliding my palm down, and grabbed his belt. I pulled him behind me. I shimmied up the stairs, eager for his hands to be on my body. I led him to my room, undressing as I went. I could hear him unfasten his belt from behind. I turned the light on, bathing us in white light. I blinked a couple of times, trying to get used to the brightness. I sat on the edge of the bed, watching and waiting.

His skin pulled taut against his defined abs as he reached for the hem of his shirt and pulled it up and over his head. He unceremoniously tossed it on the floor. I continued to watch, entranced with the incredibly toned physique before me. He kicked his pants and briefs off. He stalked toward me with powerful thighs. I smiled and bit down on my lower lip with anticipation. His athletic build became the perfect eye candy as he neared. I scanned his torso until I found my favorite piece. His cock at full mast was average and thin.

Oh, shit. I was going to be stabbed with a needle. I

never made fun of a penis but his was actually disappointing. My excitement immediately took a nosedive. I must have masked my disappointment well because he climbed up the bed and nestled between my legs. The weight of him on top of me reignited some of the lost desire. I decided to throw caution to the wind. He may not be packing below but he very well could know how to use it.

I reached over, pulled out a condom from my nightstand, and sheathed his barely there penis. His lips lowered to my collarbone. I angled my head away to give him more access to my most sensitive spot. He placed one gentle kiss that sent shivers down my body. I moaned with pleasure. Paying no more attention to my spot, he licked his way to my nipple. He sucked the tight bud into his mouth and then bit down harshly and slammed into my dry pussy.

I rolled my eyes toward the ceiling, praying that God would spare me more agony. He pumped in and out like a broken jackhammer barely cracking the cement. This was beyond torturous, with his sweaty body grunting as he slid in and out of me. The only thing that I felt was the irritating scrape of him thrusting. I was as dry as the Sahara at high noon. His body convulsed twice as he came. *Thank-fucking-God. That was the worst––*I turned my head toward my alarm clock––*fucking five minutes of my life.*

"That was incredible," he said, still panting.

"Yes, it was one for the books." Sarcasm dripped from my tongue.

He pecked my cheek and rolled off me to dispose of the condom. Immediately after returning to my room, he pulled on his clothing. He walked over to the bed where I had remained when he left. I hadn't bothered to even dress or pull the covers over my naked body. He bent down and placed a kiss on my forehead while his hand tweaked my nipple.

"I'll see you later."

I lay there, too stunned to move or utter a word. That selfish prick never even thought to make sure that I had gotten off. I could overlook his terrible fucking if he had at least gone down on me. Then again, the way he attacked my breast made me cringe and feel afraid for my clit. Nothing in that entire encounter screamed rematch. That motherfucker was dead to me. I've had fuck buddies, one-night stands, and brief relationships. Not once had any of those gentlemen treated me like a blowup doll.

I never questioned how he knew where the door out was. *Come to think of it, he never asked me where the bathroom was.* I hopped out of bed and slipped on my robe. I turned on all the lights on my way to the door that led to the backstairs leading to the parking lot. It was unlocked. We didn't come up this way and I know I had locked it when I left to meet Marie. When I got to work, I went through the front door of the bar. I quickly turned the deadbolt and dashed to the stairs that led to the bar. It was locked. *Phew!* I stared at it, confused. *Fuck it.* This night was ruined and I wouldn't think of him again.

MACK 7

I HAD PLANNED ON GOING TO the Hickey and talk with my little Ruby but Riley took precedence. She had demanded all of my attention. Not even a piece of tail would tear me away from this precious little girl.

"It's time foe my bath, Unci Mack." Riley looked up at me with her pretty doe-eyed look.

"I think that is your mommy's job." I glanced over at Candice. Her chuckles were icing on the cake. Damn that woman. She wasn't going to help me out. Of course, Forrest, my so-called best friend, had clamped his mouth shut as well.

"No. I got get my bathing suit. You give me a bath." She stomped up the stairs to where I presumed her bedroom was and screamed down, "Come on, Unci Mack. You need to won my bath while I get my suit on. K."

I seared my friends with a death ray of a look. They only laughed harder.

"You heard our princess. You better get up there before she floods the bathroom with the tub water," Forrest smarted.

My chair scraped against the hardwood as I made a mad dash for the stairs. I took them two at a time, rushing toward the bathroom. No way was I going to clean up a flooded bathroom. Blessedly, the bathroom was empty of Riley. I turned on the bath water and waited for the queen to arrive. With dramatic flair, she waltzed in.

"I gwabbed my pony. He is filthy. Can he take a bath with me?"

"Sure, squirt. Toss him in and we will clean him up too."

Her mega-watt grin had my heart ping-ponging in my chest. She could bring down an army with her smile. I hoped that one day I had a daughter as sweet and as funny as she was.

The water had turned cold and Riley shivered. I picked up her shivering body and wrapped her in her Disney towel. I reached into the cold water for Peanut, her horse, and swaddled him in a washcloth. I sat on the lid of the toilet and combed her wet ringlets. There was no way I was putting on her pajamas. I had to draw the line somewhere. She had conned me into this much. I took her towel and threw it in the hamper while she claimed her favorite PJs. I carried her downstairs and promptly handed her off to her mother.

The whole right side of my body was sopping wet from her bathing suit.

"Your turn."

I swatted Forrest on the back of the head on my way to grabbing a beer. I believe the occasion called for it. With my beer in my hand, I walked out to the porch. I slumped in the Adirondack chair and shot-gunned the beer down. *Fuck me, that tasted good.*

Forrest sat next to me. "Have you thought anymore about partnering with me?"

"You want me to be your partner? I thought you'd be the boss." I took another swig, only for it to be empty.

"Nope. I want us to be fifty-fifty in this." He took a long gulp. "I had the papers drawn up right after you left."

"How'd you know that I would come back?" I questioned, more than a little taken back.

"I didn't. I only hoped."

I nodded, satisfied with his answer. I wasn't completely surprised. One of Forrest's best qualities was his ability to read people. He knew your steps before you even moved a foot.

The sliding door swung open and banged against the doorstop. We both swung our heads in the direction.

"Unci Mack, will you wead me a bedtime stowy?"

"You got it, squirt." I stood, ready to follow Riley in. I twisted around back toward Forrest. "I'm in." I caught his shit-eating grin before I headed after Riley.

Three thick books later, Riley finally drifted off. I pulled the comforter around her and snuck out of her room, making sure not to wake her. With the house quiet, I headed to my room. She had worn me out. I stepped out of my damp clothing and slid under the covers. Sleep came quickly.

I was up and pounding the pavement before anyone else had stirred. Running when the streets were bare and the bustle of the town was far from beginning offered me the peace to clear my head. I ran mile after mile, coming to a stop in front of the door to the Hickey. The bar was dark and silent. I walked around the building to the back. A set of stairs summoned me. I jogged up the short flight to another door. I hoped that this was my little Ruby's door. I never gave it a thought that it might belong to someone else. A split second passed as I made up my mind and pounded on the door.

Beyond the door, I heard minor scuffling, along with faint curse words. *Shit, this wasn't going to go well.* The door whooshed open from the force of the wild woman behind it. She was a fucking sight. Her hair knotted around her face from sleep. She stood there in a tiny robe that was tied loosely. I wanted to claim the valley between her breasts with my tongue and taste her heaven. The sliver of her creamy skin tortured me. The need to touch every inch that lay underneath was maddening.

"Hey Ruby. Want to get breakfast?" *Yep.* I said the lamest thing that could ever pop out of my mouth. I was a certifiable douchebag.

"For fuck's sake, it's still dark out." She slammed the door in my face. "I don't eat breakfast with guys who have no name," she hollered through the pane.

As she turned her body to go, I called out, "It's Mack. Now let me in."

I didn't know what the hell I was doing but I knew that I couldn't let her walk away. The pull for her was too strong for me to deny. She had her arms folded under her breasts, driving them higher. *Fuck!* I was in trouble. My dick stirred to life. Her body tormented mine.

"How about I cook breakfast while you go back and lay in bed? I don't want anything in return. I only want to spend time with you." *That didn't sound creepy at all! Not.*

Through the glass, her body vibrated with silent laughter. Her arms swung away from her body as she reached for the door handle. "That right there tipped the scales on the creepy factor. You know that, right?"

I laughed at my stupidity. Fabio I was not. Usually, I was more suave then this. This feisty woman had me all torn up and I had only met her once. Stranger shit has happened.

"Yeah. As soon as I said it, I wanted to bitch slap myself. Seriously, though. You go back to bed and relax and I will drum up some breakfast."

Her head cocked to the side, trying to decide whether she wanted to trust me or not. She could. If I wanted to, I could have silently slipped in without her even knowing it but that definitely went in to serious stalker territory. A stalker I was not. A horny bastard——that I was and I wanted her.

"I can't believe I am doing this." She shook her head as she opened the door and let me pass through. "I'm going back to bed. Everything you need to make yourself something to eat is in the fridge or cupboard. Make yourself at home."

She pointed to the cupboards on her way out. I'd take what I could get. I was a stranger and she let me in her home. She either felt safe or I didn't give off the murderous vibe.

"Thanks."

She waved the back of her hand in the air, dismissing me. Damn, I loved a sassy woman. I bet she was a hellcat in the bedroom.

I opened up the fridge and glanced at the contents. It was well stocked. I took out the eggs and sausage. She had some red pepper and Swiss cheese. I snatched those too. I diced the peppers and put them in my egg mixture. I searched her cupboards for some garlic powder and Greek seasoning. I spotted them and dumped a healthy dose into the bowl. I scrambled up the mixture, making sure all the ingredients were properly mixed. I twisted the knob and listened to the *click, click* of the gas igniting. I poured the mixture into the pan and went to work on heating the sausage.

I divided up the food onto two plates. I didn't see a tray so I carried both plates. I set one on the kitchen table and continued with the other one. I peeked in the bedroom with the door open; the bed was empty. I walked down the hall to the door that was closed.

I rapped lightly. "Abbie, I have your plate. Would you like me to set it on the floor or bring it in to you?"

"You can come in."

I opened the door with my free hand. I hoped that she slept in the nude and would offer me a bit of her glorious body. She sat up in bed, still in her flimsy excuse of a robe. Naked would have been better but this would do, for now. The soft glow of her bedside lamp set her red locks afire. She was temptation at its finest.

I walked over to her side and set the plate on her nightstand. "I'm going to eat mine at the table. I'll clean up before I head out."

Surprise flashed quickly across her face before she masked it. "I'll be out in a minute and eat with you."

I smiled, hoping that she would do just that. If I spent any more time this close to her half-naked body, I would eat her for breakfast. "I'll wait for you."

I grabbed her plate and brought it to the table. I poured us both some juice and sat in the chair like a gentlemen and waited. In the three minutes it took her to sit across from me, I had envisioned taking her a thousand different ways.

I watched her delicately insert the fork past her kissable lips. Blood flooded to my cock. Her soft moan had my dick at full mast. That was the sexiest thing I've ever seen and heard in my entire life. I pushed on my dick with my hand, trying to alleviate the pressure. *So not working.* She opened her eyes and caught me staring.

"Shit. Did I moan out loud?" Her cheeks instantly colored.

I cleared my throat. "I hope to hell you moan like that with every bite."

She shook her head with embarrassment.

"I must warn you that if you continue with those wicked sounds, I'm going to toss you on top of this table and make you scream."

I meant every word, too. I had a limited amount of control at the moment. Especially when her nipples stood erect and begged for my attention.

"So, Mack, what brings you to my door this early in the morning?" she asked, effectively changing the subject.

"I was out running. When I stopped, it happened to be in front of your bar. I walked around back and noticed the stairs. I figured, what the hell, see if she is home and wanted to get a bite to eat." I stuffed some sausage in my mouth. When I swallowed, I finished my thought. "So I knocked, hoping that you lived here and not some old lady."

"What if I had someone with me? Did you ever think of that?"

Nope, I sure didn't. "I would have figured that out when I encountered it." I was pretty quick on my feet. I could finagle my way out of almost every situation.

"What are you going to do with the rest of your day?" she asked sincerely.

"Not sure. All depends on how motivated I feel."

"I'd say that anyone who got up to run this fucking early in the morning would be highly driven."

I openly guffawed. "You are a smart woman."

Her smile was genuine and radiant. "So I've been told."

I stood and collected her empty plate along with mine. I washed them and put them on the counter to dry. She had walked up behind me and leaned her back against the counter. I had the urge to pick her up and wrap her legs around me. I resisted the temptation and finished the task at hand. I had already barged into her home. I wasn't going to push my way into her pussy. However, I did cage her against the counter with my body.

Her face was seemingly unaffected. Yet, her breathing came in short bursts. Her breasts heaved up and down heavily. Her nipples poked my chest, begging me to play. My cock pushed against my sweatpants, letting her know the effect she had on me. I bent my head down as she angled hers up, her silent challenge accepted.

I placed my finger under her chin, holding her right where I wanted her. I gently sucked her bottom lip into my mouth, letting my tongue slide along the plump flesh. She opened for me and my tongue swept inside, tangling with hers. She wrapped her arms around my neck as I pushed my cock harder against her warmth. This felt way too good. I slowed the kiss before she took me to the place of no return.

"Thank you for breakfast. Tomorrow morning? Same time?" I practically growled.

"More like tonight after closing."

I winked. "I'll be at the door waiting," I whispered along her neck.

Goose bumps erupted along her delicate neck. I smiled as I turned away and walked out the door.

ABBIE 8

WHEN THE DOOR CLICKED BACK into place, I let out a shaky breath. Mack was more lethal than a PMS, coffee-withdrawn, spurned woman. He could cut you to the quick with his tongue, make you quake with obsession, and own your soul in a matter of seconds. I had the urge to barricade my door and hide under the covers. He had a dark side that hovered around the edges, waiting to be unleashed. I wanted to be there when his darkness unfurled its claws. He would tear my mischievous soul to shreds and I would enjoy every minute of it.

I would only toss and turn if I tried to go back to sleep. Mack had engaged every one of my senses; shutting them down now would be worthless. I put some old clothes on, brushed my teeth, threw my hair in a ponytail, and headed down to the bar. Now would be the perfect time to check inventory. With the clipboard in my hand, I scribbled down what needed to be ordered and what needed to be locally purchased. A Sam's trip was on the horizon. Because I was up this early, my premium membership would get me through the doors prior to the huge rush that would come mid-afternoon. I tore the paper from the pad and set the clipboard on the bar. I would finish the liquor inventory later. I was on a mission to beat the crowd.

I found a parking spot right next to where you return the shopping carts. I hated to have to run the cart back into the store if there wasn't a close one. I couldn't leave one left stranded for some poor schmuck's car to get dinged. The vast majority of people do not do this; they just leave the damn thing out there to cause damage. I pulled out my membership card before I opened the car door. When I chose to throw caution to the wind and reach for it once I got through the doors, it was never easy to find. Then I became the jackass who stood for ten minutes while the line of angry people grew behind me. That made it worse and the card nearly impossible to find. Stepping out of line would be a must until I found the damn thing. So, today I did the sensible thing and placed it in my pocket before I even reached the store's entrance.

I whipped the membership card out of my pocket and flashed her my membership like a pro. I breezed by the card lady. I took the list out of my other pocket and started to look for the items. I didn't have to wander down any aisles to find the supplies I needed. I had been coming to this store for years. They hadn't really changed anything. Most of the items were all in the same aisles as they were when I was a kid, hanging off my dad's arm.

With the cart fully stuffed, I checked out, and was quickly packing the back end of my car. The great thing about this place was that I could take half of the product that was packaged in bulk and replace what I needed in my apartment. I slammed the trunk shut and put the pesky cart away.

"Abbie?"

I spun around to face the voice that called my name.

Oh, fucking great. "Hi, Travis. How are you doing?" What I really wanted to do was pretend that I didn't hear my name and peel out of the parking lot, far away from him. He wasn't a bad guy. I simply did not want a repeat. The only thing that sucked about small-town living was avoiding one-night stands that would never have a chance of a repeat. Hence, the phrase: one-night stand.

"Great. I'm glad I ran into you. I want to see you again. Are you busy tonight?" A hopeful gleam twinkled in his eyes.

Yeah, so not happening. He needed to find some college chick to hook up with. "I'm sorry, Travis. Tonight isn't a good night. Maybe some other time?" I looked at my watch pointedly. "I have to get going. See you around."

I turned on my heel so fast that a piercing pain shot through my ankle. I steadily kept my course and hopped into my car. I ignored the pain as I slammed on the gas and drove the fuck away. I didn't look back, either; only thanked my lucky stars that no one had parked in front of me. Escaping his presence was the only thing on my mind. I wasn't even remotely interested and didn't want to give him false hopes. I don't like clingers either, and that's exactly what his body language was telling me. Plus, his bedroom skills were less than desirable. I didn't have the energy or the desire to coach him. I had a date with Mack and right now that's all I wanted. I didn't want Travis to taint that. Mack's visit had erased last night's debacle. I was all for him making me forget Travis's name. Hell, he would probably make me forget my own. I could feel the wicked smile form on my lips. The eagerness of tonight had my body humming with desire.

Once all of the items were stored, I grabbed my phone and dialed Marie.

"Holy shit, girl," I panted out.

"Just breathe and tell me what's up." She easily settled my frantic thoughts.

"You're never going to believe this one."

"Try me!" she butted in.

"Mack knocked on my door bright and early this morning."

"He didn't?" she screamed into the mouthpiece.

I pulled the phone away from my ear and put her on speaker. Her shrieking would blow out my eardrum. "Shut up and let me finish."

"Fine. Speak."

I chuckled, understanding her impatience. "Yeah. So, he knocks on my door. At first I thought it was Travis."

"Who the hell is Travis? I thought we were talking about Mack," she huffed out, confused.

"I am. If you'll keep quiet long enough, you'll find out."

"All right. This is me, not saying another word."

I could hear her pacing around her kitchen. The smacking of her flip-flops hit the tile in a rhythmic motion. She couldn't stand or sit in one spot for long, especially if she was neck-deep in gossip.

"Travis was the guy I had slept with last night. Just some guy from the bar I picked up. He happened to be the worst lay in history. Regardless, after he left, I tossed and turned until the wee hours, completely worked up. I had finally dozed as the sun had come up. No sooner did I close my eyes when I heard a knock at the door. I thought it was Travis coming back but when I looked out the door, it was Mack. I was still pissed from not reaching my O that I really didn't give a shit if he came in or went away." I took a huge breath and then plugged on. "I let him in and went back to bed."

"No you didn't. I know you better than that. Curiosity burned behind your lids, girl."

I sighed heavily. "He said he was hungry and wanted

to make me breakfast. Shit, girl. He was all sweaty from a run and I wanted to lick him from head to toe."

"Please tell me that he was the one doing all the licking."

I rolled my eyes; she lived for this kind of stuff. "I'm telling you I showed him where everything was and I went and hid under the covers. He knocked on my door and when I let him in, he was carrying a plate of food for me."

"You are a big fat liar!"

"I'm dead serious. He put it on my nightstand and left to go eat his at the table. He didn't try anything. I walked out of the room and sat down opposite from him and ate breakfast with him. Hell girl, he even cleaned up both plates."

"That's it. No kissing, banging––only innocent stuff went on?"

I could hear the disbelief in her voice.

"He did kiss me and told me he would see me tonight."

"What? No freaking way. Is he a good kisser?" She spoke in high pitches.

"Made my toes curl. He knows what he is doing with his mouth, that's for sure."

"Oh my God! Tell me you are going to take him to bed and use his delicious body for impure things."

I giggled. "You bet your scandalous thoughts, I am."

"That's my girl. You better call me tomorrow."

"You know I will."

"If you don't, you know that I'll psycho call you until you pick up."

"All right. I have to go finish up some stuff before I open. I'll call you tomorrow. Luv ya, bye."

"Luv ya, too."

I hung up, feeling giddier than I did before. Not that

I needed her to amp me up even more but she always had my back. She never once called or thought of me as a slut for being cavalier with men. I loved the dynamics of our friendship. There was no judgment from either side. We accepted each other as we were. There were no pretenses or back stabbing between us. When we were pissed at each other, we didn't pull any punches. We said exactly what was on our minds. We were honest and loyal and that was priceless to me. I didn't want a friend who would demean me behind my back or sugarcoat life when I needed to hear the hard truth.

I plugged in the jukebox and let the eighties singers croon through the speakers. Tonight would be a packed house. We had a local band playing the stage. Broken Down was the name of their band and they mostly sang cover songs. Their wide range of songs drew the crowds in. They could sing anything and very well. I'm genuinely surprised that they haven't been picked up for a record deal yet. The guys didn't seem interested in one. They all had families, with the exception of Brett, and held regular jobs. This was mainly their hobby.

Matt was a pediatric doctor and had married his high school sweetheart, Lana. They had a ten-year-old little girl named Emma. She was the most tenderhearted young lady that I have ever had the pleasure of meeting. After Emma went to school fulltime, Lana finished her degree in teaching. She now teaches a rowdy bunch of five-year-olds and loves every minute of it. Lana was as down-to-earth as Matt was. They made an incredible pair.

Thomas rocked a beer gut and has been married to Trudy for over twenty years. He owned the detail shop north of town. He offers me a free car detail every time I stop in. Which isn't that often. I don't like to take advantage of his generous offer. Trudy works at the courthouse as an administrative assistant. She has been contemplating retiring for the last five years. Knowing her, she would stay there until they force her out.

Scotty was newly married to Hanna. I had gone to school with her and she was mostly quiet. I didn't know her very well but she beams at him throughout their whole set when they play at the bar. They were totally gross to watch together. Yet, I secretly wanted what they had, just not sure if it was for me.

Brett was the most handsome of the bunch. He had recently gone through a divorce. Last month, I thought the ladies were going to riot when they learned that he was now single. I had to kick some of the "friendlier" ones out. Brett was on the fire department and looked damn good in his uniform. I made sure to buy the fundraising calendar ever year. When I had met him, he was still married so I never thought about him in that way but that didn't stop me from getting an eyeful of his luscious body.

They were pretty popular in town and the neighboring cities. They were often booked for weddings and reunions. Broken Down was one of my favorite bands that played on my stage. They were one of the first bands that I had asked to play regularly. No one had a contract when they played here. It was always up to them if they wanted to continue the gig. The anticipation of seeing Mack and hearing my favorite band had me feeling slightly lightheaded. Tonight would be epic, or so I had high hopes that it would.

I swiped my lips with red-valentine lipstick. The deep-red hue matched the retro chic I had planned for tonight's attire. The nineteen forties pinup style was the fashion that I chose when I worked. Outside of the bar, it was mostly anything that I could find clean. Even the thought of washing clothes had me cringing with distaste. I wrapped and pinned a scarf around the top of my head to complete my look. I locked up the apartment and headed downstairs to open.

Within the two hours of being open, I had yet to spot Mack. I hated to seem eager and I couldn't help but stare at the door, waiting for him to come. With each patron who came through, a little of my hope disappeared. *Damn, now I was becoming a clinger.* Time to focus on the band and the rest of my clientele. Pining for something that might not even happen had me feeling disgusted with myself. I looked fucking hot tonight and if Mack wasn't here to appreciate it, well, I had enough invites to choose from.

The boys had arrived shortly after eight to begin setting up. *Thank God for distractions.*

I gave each of the boys a hug. "How are ya'll doing tonight?"

They all gave a chorus of *fine, good, and can't complain.* I laughed with them and took their drink orders.

"I'll be right back, boys."

I went behind the bar and grabbed a bucket of their favorite beer.

I turned to Eddy. "Hey, do me a favor and make sure that you keep the band's bucket filled."

Eddy was my only steady employee. He was a little older than me and only slightly cuter. He appealed to the ladies and I appealed to the men. My dad had hired him shortly before he had passed away. We got along like siblings. I hired two bar-backs to help on the weekends. They happened to be in their mid-twenties, twins, and going to the university in town. Jory was petite and yet fierce. I'm not sure whether she was making up for her lack of height with attitude but it worked for her. She was a sight to behold. Her lithe body and sassy mouth won the men over. Her brother Mason was taller than her and wiry. The girls thought that he was the most innocent young man to grace the bar, which had scored him many dates. Quite the opposite in fact; I'm sure his list of women was a mile long. I didn't know what they had planned for the future. For now they enjoyed their weekend hours and so did I.

"You got it, boss."

"Thanks," I hollered over my shoulder as I set two buckets on the window ledge at the back of the stage. "Here you go. If you need anything at all, just holler."

"Thanks, Abbie," they mumbled as they tuned their instruments, having already forgotten my presence.

The first notes of "Roadhouse Blues" by the Doors drifted through the place and livened up the crowd. Heads started to bob and fingers began to tap the bar. When the guys finished up the song, a round of cheers rose up. A quick thank-you from Brett and they were on to the next song. "Sweet Home Alabama" began to play and the bar went wild. Off-key singing could be heard from every patron. *Damn, they weren't pulling any punches tonight.* They had the beginnings of an incredible set. They wouldn't disappoint tonight—or any night they played, for that matter.

I lost track of time during the first half of their set. They took a break and I was able to breathe and relax a little. The drinking slowed as the boys made their rounds, talking to everyone who stopped by their table. I checked in with everyone behind the bar, making sure to restock what we were low on, and to give every employee their break. I found a rare moment and went to chat with the boys.

As I sat there, strong hands landed on my shoulders. The rough, callused fingers kneaded my tight muscles. My head involuntarily tilted back and into a hard-lined abdomen. I looked upward and spotted the scar first. My pulse quickened at the sight of Mack. His chiseled bone structure looked fierce and predatory. I closed my eyes for a moment, trying to control my raging hormones. I sat straighter in my chair and made the necessary introductions.

"Matt, Brett, Scotty, and Thomas––this is Mack. He is a friend of mine."

His skilled hands left my shoulders to shake the hands of the band members.

I stood. "Here, take my seat. I need to get back behind the bar. Whiskey neat?"

His eyes drank me in from head to toe before he answered. "Please."

"You got it."

I had to get away from him. Holy hell, he was intoxicating. I felt drunk being in his presence even though I hadn't had a drop of alcohol. I helped Eddy catch up before I made his drink. I could have had Jory take it to him but I wanted to do that myself. I needed another fix before I got stuck behind here.

I walked over and set his drink on the table. "Catch you later. Enjoy these guys. They are the best." I winked and sashayed back to my spot.

I could feel his eyes on me the entire time. It was both exhilarating and unnerving. I held most of the control when it came to men. No man before Mack could unsettle me this way. Not even when I was with Gage. Gage was sexy and had turned me on but being around Mack had me close to self-combustion.

MACK 9

I SAT IN THE CHAIR WITH a hard-on that wouldn't quit. My little Ruby was a pinup gem. She looked wicked and smelled sultry. The moment I had laid eyes on her, my dick had made an appearance. You couldn't tell by my casual posture that beneath my skin my blood boiled, brewing up a storm of epic proportions. I couldn't wait for the band to end their set and the bar to close down. My body was sprung tight with need for the tantalizing redhead. I could hear her sweet laughter from across the bar. Her scent went straight to my head and drove me wild.

I looked toward the ceiling as the lights flashed bright in the dim atmosphere. Last call had finally arrived. One more hour, and my hands and mouth would be suckling every inch of her skin. The band had quit playing and sat back down at the table. I shot the shit with them for the remainder of the night. They were a funny group of guys. I especially got along well with Thomas. He reminded me of what I had wanted my father to be.

I kept stock-still until every person had vacated. Abbie turned the Open sign off and locked the door. She flipped the main switch for the lights off. A dim light from behind the bar remained on, casting the two of us in shadow of darkness. She stood with her back against the door with her hands behind her back.

"Come here," I gritted out. I was losing control with each passing second.

Her long legs ate up the space between us. She stood before me, soaking up every detail. I placed my hands on the sides of her bare thighs. I ran them up toward her hip and back down. I opened my legs and pulled her between them so I could reach more of her creamy skin. Desire rolled off her in heated waves. Euphoria clouded my brain.

I placed my mouth above her tiny shorts and licked the sliver of skin that had played peek-a-boo with me all night. She tossed her head back with a breathless moan. I grabbed her hips tightly and lifted her off the ground, moving her onto my lap. Her heat blanketed my cock, causing it to grow to the point of blissful pain. I had never wanted to be inside a woman this desperately.

I dragged my hands from her delicious ass up her back and around her shoulders. She arched into me as I relieved her of her top and bra. Fuck, she was gorgeous. Her tits were more than a handful. Her hardened nipples were within licking distance. I popped one of her peaked nipples into my mouth. I used my tongue to lash at the hardened bud. She pushed her breast farther into my mouth, needing more. I scraped my teeth along her sensitive peak.

"Mack, please. I need more," she panted.

"And I will give you so much more."

I picked her up as I stood. She wrapped her muscular thighs around me.

"I hope your door is open." I barely formed the sentence. Her lips had attached themselves to my neck and were doing delicious things to my overly heated skin.

Her husky laugh had my cock twitching with urgency.

"Nope."

"I'll break this fucker down before you reach for your key."

She kept right on lavishing my neck, unconcerned about her door. I wasn't playing around. I was so fucking hard for her that a pesky lock would not hold me back. When I hit the top stair, I asked again. "Do you have your key?"

Her tongue momentarily left its spot. "Downstairs in my purse."

"Fuck it. I'll replace it in the morning. Hang on, sweetheart."

She wrapped her limbs around me tighter. I kicked out my leg. The force of my first kick fractured the wood around the lock. She gasped when my second kick splintered the rest of the wood and the door flung open. I looked up in to her rosy face. Her swollen lips practically begged me to shove my cock inside. Shock at what I had done slipped from her gaze and a molten heat that I had never seen before took its place. She attacked me as though we were the last species on earth and in our final hours.

I banged into multiple furnishings on our way toward her bedroom. I would've fucked her in the bar but there was still time for that. I wanted her spread out on her bed the first time I took her. This wasn't going to be a fast fuck no matter what my dick thought. I pried the little hellcat from my body and tossed her on the bed. The way her tits bounced up and down as she landed almost had me squirting in my pants.

"Take your shorts off but leave your panties on," I commanded.

She did as she was told.

"Good girl. Now raise your arms above your head.

Make sure your fingers touch the headboard and spread your legs."

Heat flooded her eyes as she maneuvered her body the way I had instructed. I ate her up with my eyes. Her polka-dotted briefs were completely soaked with her desire. As I took in her curves, I wrestled with the urge to plunge into her warm center. Worshiping her was my only objective. My own release would come but not yet. The need to extract every drop of her desire overrode my primitive demands.

Her eyes, wide like saucers, were glued to my every move. She soaked in every inch of my skin as I stripped. My dick grew harder from the lust that swirled around her. Her body involuntarily squirmed. I enjoyed watching her struggle to stay in one position as turned on as she was.

I took my time climbing on the bed between her creamy thighs.

"Exquisite."

She whimpered when my lips gently kissed along her calf, licking up her inner thigh. I placed gentle kisses along her covered mound and followed down the other leg. I placed my hands on each ankle and spread her wider.

"Please, Mack," she panted.

"Please, what?"

"Touch me."

"Touch you here?" I grazed my fingers along the arch of her heel. I continued lapping up her leg with my mouth, inching my way closer to her pussy.

She shook her head back and forth as though she were possessed.

"Tell me where you want me to touch you and I will be more than happy to."

"I want you to put your tongue on my clit and your fingers in my pussy." She took a deep breath, trying to regain control over her body.

"With pleasure."

I took the waistband of her panties with both of my hands and tore the one side. I did the same with the other side and let the pesky material fall away. Her sweet and salty musk beckoned me closer.

With her completely open, I dipped my tongue between her folds, and licked my way to her bundle of nerves. I swirled my tongue around the hard nub and then inserted two fingers. Her hips came off the bed and pushed her clit harder against my tongue. I gently restrained her hips so she couldn't move. I was the only one who would give her this pleasure and at my pace. I curled my fingers inside her and massaged her g-spot. I flattened my tongue and licked my way from her opening to her clit. Her inner muscles tightened around my fingers.

"Fuck. I'm coming," she screamed.

Her pussy contracted and her hips bucked wildly as she came. Her sweet taste glistened around my mouth and I couldn't get enough. I kept pumping my fingers in and out of her channel.

"Can't get enough," I hummed.

"Oh, God. Mack, I can't take anymore."

"Yes, you can and you will."

I pulled my drenched fingers from her pussy and brought them to my mouth. I sucked off her essence. "Tastes so damn good."

"Fuck me. I need you inside so bad."

I chuckled and licked my pinky finger. I inserted my two fingers into her still pulsating core as her muscles gripped around me. I pushed past her button hole. I fucked her pussy with my fingers, mouth, and made sure to fill her ass.

"Holy shit. It's too much."

Her toes curled and she came again, screaming my name. I could get off from the sounds that rolled off her tongue while she was in the throes of an orgasm. I kissed my way up her stomach and latched onto her hardened nipple. I drew the dusty rosebud into my mouth and suckled as I pinched and tweaked the other one between the tips of my fingers. She wrapped her arms around my neck and dug her fingernails deep into my skin. There would be marks and I couldn't wait for the sting of them to hit tomorrow.

I kissed my way up her chest to the delicate skin of her neck. Her petite moans made my dick reach for her entrance. I nipped at her ear and down her jaw to her luscious lips. They were puffy and red from her biting at them each time she came. I pushed her lips a part and plunged my tongue inside. My tongue mated with hers while my dick was poised against her folds await-ing access. She wrapped her firm legs around my waist, signaling the green light. I thrust my hips and drove my cock into her tight pussy. I groaned from the exquisite sensation. Her silky muscles drew me in and seduced my cock. At this rate I wasn't going to last long. She tight-ened around me and I was gone.

I rolled to my side and brought her to my chest.

"Fuck. I didn't use a condom."

Her head shot up as my words sunk in.

I peered into her forest-colored eyes. "Please tell me you are on the pill."

"That's a real romantic thing to say."

Her frustrated sigh ricocheted through my bones. I didn't mean to come off as an asshole. I was pissed at myself for forgetting to put one on. *I never forget.*

I placed a tiny kiss on her forehead. "I'm sorry. That came out more harsh than I had intended."

"It's okay. I am on the pill. I was just as caught up. I'm clean."

She peeked at me from under her eyelashes. The question in her eyes was clear.

"I'm clean."

She put her head upon my chest, mollified. Her breathing evened out while I lay there regulating my own. Her hand lay limp over my heart as she succumbed to sleep. I closed my eyes and followed shortly after.

My internal clock woke me well before the sun could rise. Even in the dark room I could perfectly see the outline of her features. Her leg had twisted itself around mine, anchoring me to her. I could've easily slipped from her human chain but I honestly didn't have the desire to move. My body began to hum from the feel of her breast teasing my ribcage. With every breath she took, her breast moved along my skin. The movement could've only been about a millimeter but every inch of skin on my side burned from the innocent caress. I bet if I woke her now that she would be eager for round two. I certainly was. I'd wait for the sun to poke through with its first rays before I claimed her again. She would need her energy, especially for what I had in mind.

Tiny slivers of light poked through her closed shades. Dust particles floated in and out of the rays, generating a chaotic rhythm. Lying beside her, I listened to her breath throughout the stillness of the morning hours. It came as a comforting surprise. I enjoyed the way her body fit perfectly into my side, as though she were merely an extension of me.

By now I would be finding something physical to

occupy my time. I don't lie in bed all morning. At first light, I was up, and usually out on my morning run. Even though I was no longer carrying one hundred plus pounds on my back in the sweltering desert heat, I maintained my physical stamina from my army days. It was a hard habit to break. I had breathed red, white, and blue for so long that I couldn't function any other way. Breaking into civilian life was fucking hard. I no longer fit in with what society dictated. Holding down a regular nine-to-five job had become torturous. It's no wonder that when the organization recruited me, I jumped at the chance. I hadn't regretted my choice. It all had led me to this point.

I slowly slipped from her embrace and crept from the room. I surveyed the damage that I had caused. The door would need to be replaced. Thankfully the frame was still intact. It was an easy fix. I'd get the new door and replace it while she was working.

ABBIE 10

MY BODY HUMMED WITH ELECTRICITY while my mind remained groggy from sleep. I had no control over the molten lust that spread through my veins. It ran hot and deep. My nipples hardened the instant his tongue had suckled the peak into his skilled mouth. A moan slipped past my lips as his fingers deftly slipped between my folds.

"Mmm. So wet," he growled.

I didn't bother responding. I let my body do all the talking. He easily rolled me to my back, slipping inside my pussy as though he were made for me. I could feel every inch of him. He took his time and made sure to heighten my pleasure with an agonizingly slow pace. His body tensed above me, holding back as though it were necessary for me to find my release first. His struggle spurred my orgasm to a level beyond anything I had ever felt. My toes curled as I shoved my head deeper into the pillow. My screams echoed off the walls, sounding more like a casted-out demon during an exorcism.

I lay limply unable to summon an ounce of energy. My body jerked as Mack slid his cock from my sinfully used body. We lay there silently, trying to catch our breaths. He reached his hand over and tweaked my nipple.

"Hello, still sensitive." I batted his hand away.

He rose and placed a chaste kiss on my forehead. "I'm going to head home and go for a run. Call me later and I'll meet you after you close."

I cocked my head to the side. "I'm not sure you were good enough for a repeat."

The brow that harbored the tip of his scar rose questioningly. His eyelids became slits as he stalked toward me. He was all male and dangerous. I was unafraid, even as my body shivered. He placed both hands around the sides of my arms caging me in.

He bent his lips close to my ear as his hand drifted down and cupped my sex. He slipped two fingers inside my already slick heat. He massaged my inner muscles. I moaned as my orgasm began to build.

"Oh no, my little Ruby. You'll do well to remember whose pussy this is. It belongs to me." He took his fingers out of my aching pussy and licked my juices clean. "Tastes so good. See you tonight."

"You better get back here and finish what you started," I yelled at his retreating back.

He waved his hand in the air. "Later, Abs."

"Men," I huffed.

I could hear his smooth chuckle echo through the apartment. He was so lucky that he had an addictive dick. Otherwise, I wouldn't be seeing his fine ass again. My body was wound tighter than a six-string banjo. *Fuck.* I wanted release but wouldn't give him the satisfaction of knowing that I had to finish what he had started. Paybacks were a bitch. I would do my best to make sure he begged me to let him cum. I wrenched my sore limbs out of bed and walked stiffly to the shower.

The cold shower did nothing to cool off the steaming pile of lust that sat heavily in my nether regions. I hadn't felt this needy since––well, never. *How could one man turn me into a raging nymph?* I didn't much care for it. No man had ever held such power over me. No matter how good he could manipulate my body, I wouldn't ever give him that kind of power over me.

It's not that I didn't want to have a committed relationship. I simply didn't want to go through what my dad did when my mom passed away. Their marriage was the soul mate kind. When she passed away, a large piece of my father did as well. Once I was old enough to realize it, I watched day after day as my only parent drifted away. My mom had passed away shortly after she had delivered me. I loved being raised by my dad. Despite not having a mother figure, my dad did an excellent job. It was almost to the point that I didn't miss not having a mother. The only time it hit me was when I had spent the night at Marie's house. Some days I believed that he had waited until I was grown to go and meet her on the other side. He had raised me to be tough and to never wallow. They were both very good lessons to learn when you no longer had any family to lean on.

I rolled my eyes toward the exposed beams of the ceiling. If I had to listen to this chick sing the same song again, I was going to have to throw my towel at her. My ears hurt from her inebriated ass thinking that she could sing. To top it off, it was some Olivia Newton-John high-pitched wail. *Holy fuck me!* Somehow I will find a way to delete that song from that stupid machine or I could break it and turn the jukebox on.

"Abbie! Can you do something about that fucking twat on stage?" Curtis shouted at me.

I couldn't blame him for wanting me to do something about it. However, I would not let him call any woman a twat.

"Listen here, Curtis, and listen good. If I ever hear you call any woman a twat again, you'll be pissing through a catheter hooked to your microscopic dick. You got me?" I shoved my face in his, invading his personal bubble.

"Yeah. Sorry Abbie," he said, shrinking into himself.

"I'll take care of it."

Most customers who knew me understood that I was no pushover and could kick some ass if need be. I may be a girl but I sure as hell don't hit like one. My dad made sure of that. He knew that I wanted the bar to be mine one day and he wanted to make sure that I knew how to take care of myself. Alcohol and violence did go hand in hand. I'm thankful for the jujitsu lessons he made me go to. I continued to go twice a week even after I had earned my black belt. The classes keep me fresh and the bellicosity to a minimum. I was by no means at the top rank. I didn't have the desire or the dedication to achieve any other belt beyond the one I earned.

The woman wouldn't quit. I watched as her index finger went to start the song over again. *Nope, not going to happen.*

I stalked up to her. "Hey, how about a drink on the house?"

"But the song is starting," she whined.

Kicking my patience to a higher level. I said, "Yes and you have been up on stage for quite a while. Why don't you take a break and wet your whistle before you sing another set?"

"That sounds like a great idea. My throat is kind of dry."

With my help, she stepped off the stage and followed

me to the bar. Cheers deafened the place as the woman cleared the stage. She took a bow, thinking they were from her performance. *What a joke.* I laughed gregariously at the woman before me. I couldn't help it. I hated to make fun of her but she tipped the scale of annoyance and I had to join in on the fun.

"What can I get you?" I asked.

"A Long Island."

I nodded my head. One virgin Long Island iced tea coming right up! She'd never know the difference. This was retaliation for making me get in Curtis's face. If anything, I was loyal to my regulars. In my own way, I loved each of them. I watched her slurp the non-alcoholic beverage and chuckled at my own private joke. I went over and fist pumped Curtis to make sure we were still cool.

"You are as mean as a snake. I saw what you did." He laughed.

"We good?"

"Yep. Thanks."

"No problem."

There was no way that I would apologize for getting in his face. I wasn't sorry that I did. However, he deserved a little retribution in his honor. The drink wasn't the payback. It would be how she handled this glass and the next drink she ordered. For the remainder of the night, all drinks––unless it was a beer––would be served with a smile and no alcohol mixed in. They, of course, would be on the house. My diabolical plan didn't include swindling her. I rubbed my hands together and waited for her faux inebriated state. If she played it like I hoped she would, this night would turn out highly entertaining.

I figured that another patron would take the woman's place at the mic but so far the stage was clear and the bar was filled with only chatter. Guess no one wanted to embarrass him or herself. It's been awhile since we had someone up there that sounded like the seagull in the *Little Mermaid* movie. Karaoke was supposed to be fun, not torturous. I had thought about doing a karaoke battle. I still might introduce the idea.

I leaned into Jory so she could hear me. "Hope someone hops up there before Long Island starts singing again."

I dubbed her Long Island because I didn't know her real name.

"I know, right." She cringed.

I looked over in her direction. "Shit. She is almost out. Be right back."

"I'll take care of the stage," she called, making her way toward Mason.

I wondered what she had up her sleeve. She was resourceful. So whatever she came up with would be good.

I took the empty glass from Long Island and replaced it with another non-alcohol filled tea.

"Thanks." She hiccupped.

I giggled as I twisted the cap off of a Coors Light and handed it to Curtis. "On the house."

He smiled. "Thanks."

Giving away free drinks was not my MO. I rarely did, even for my regulars. Can't run a profitable business with free drinks. Tonight, I was feeling a little generous——or guilty. I preferred generous. I walked up and down the bar and made sure every person was taken care of. Eddy was out working the tables so I stayed clear. A table full of middle-aged women was vying for his attention. He was eating that shit up. His pockets would be fat tonight.

My ears perked when I heard Mason calling out, "This next song to all the ladies." *What the hell was he doing up there?* This should be interesting. His hands tapped his leg with the tune of the song. He belted out the lyrics to "Mustang Sally" and I about creamed my panties. His bluesy vocals seemed too big for his sinewy physique. His voice had all the ladies, including myself, swooning as he crooned each lyric. I leaned up against the bar, entranced. When the song ended, he had earned a standing ovation. We all chanted "Encore!" until he laughed and did another song. We made sure to keep him up on the stage for three more songs. He finally shook his head and stepped off the stage. No doubt that his bed would be full tonight.

He stepped behind the bar and grabbed a towel to wipe the sweat off his face. I grabbed him and pulled him into a tight hug.

"Holy shit, college boy. I had no idea you had such pipes!"

"If that's all I had to do to get your attention, I would've done it sooner." He laughed and slapped me on the ass.

"Whatever, big boy. Watch those hands." I giggled.

He was a huge flirt and so was I. This was purely innocent fun. He was no more into me than I was into him. Jory ran over and inserted herself in to our embrace. I truly loved these two.

"You were awesome. I knew you'd blow them away!" She squeezed us.

"Thanks." He blushed.

"I think that you should play once a month. I'd give you one weekend a month off if you would play on a regular Saturday."

His eyes lit up. "Really?"

"Yep." I turned toward Jory. "Do you sing as well?"

"I wish. I can't sing any better than Long Island over there." She laughed.

"Well, shit. I guess you are stuck behind the bar with

me."

"No skin off my back." She chuckled.

"All right, off you go. Back to work."

The rest of the night seemed to fly by after Mason sang. More and more customers grabbed the mic and sang. Most of them weren't bad either. The occasional voice grated my nerves but they were one song and done. Nothing like my pretend-drunk Long Island. She hadn't had a sip of alcohol for about three hours and yet she was falling off the stool and stumbling to and from the bathroom. Every single time I saw her, I laughed and winked at Curtis.

I dimmed the lights and shouted last call. The bar had already pretty much thinned out. There were only a few stragglers. I started wiping down the empty tables. I was bent over one, cleaning, when a pair of hands went around my waist. They pulled me flush with their pelvis. I could feel his hard cock on my ass. The hair on the back of my neck stood up. The creep vibe wound its way around my body. I didn't have to turn around to know that it was Travis. I don't know why I didn't notice it when he was fucking me but I sure as hell did now.

"Let's go upstairs after you close. I've been watching you for the past ten minutes and you've got me rock hard." He spoke close to my ear.

I stood to my full height and twisted out of his grip. "Travis, I don't appreciate you manhandling me."

"I wasn't manhandling you. I thought we had a good time the other night." His features bordered on a sneer.

"Yeah, you did. I, on the other hand, did not. I'd appreciate it if you didn't grab me again like we were some couple. We fucked one time. That, in my book, does not mean I have to fuck you again."

He stood there with an almost vacant look in his eye.

Which made me more eager to get far away from him.

Mason walked up beside me. "Is this guy bothering you, Abbie?"

"Nah, Mason. He was just leaving. Right, Travis?"

He finally looked at me instead of through me. "Right. I was just saying good-bye to Abbie. See you around."

I blew out a breath. "Thanks for having my back, Mason. He isn't right in the head. I don't think he will be back again. I made it pretty clear that I don't want anything to do with him."

He winked at me. "You need to be more selective when you pick your bed partners."

I slapped his shoulder. "You're just jealous that I've never had you in my bed."

His body shook with laughter. "If you weren't my boss, I'd have already had you in my bed."

"Yeah, okay, Casanova." I rolled my eyes.

Once the bar cleared out, I shut and locked the door. Eddy and I stayed an extra hour to get the place cleaned up. I had sent Jory and Mason home earlier.

I walked Eddy to the door. "See you Wednesday. Enjoy the next couple of days off."

I relocked the door and headed to my apartment. I inserted the key but the lock wouldn't turn. It was then that I noticed an envelope wedged between the door and the frame. I carefully slid the envelope out. I opened the flap, curious to see the contents. Two keys lay in the corner pocket. I pulled one out and tried the lock. The bolt slid back with ease. I don't know how he snuck around me but that sly fox installed a new door for me. A cheesy grin spread along my face. That man was full of surprises. I walked to my bedroom and shucked my clothes, eager to put on something more comfortable. I slipped my robe on to hide my nakedness. A loud knock from the front door could be heard all the way to my bedroom.

I looked through the glass. *Just the man I wanted to see.* I took my time walking toward the door. I didn't want him think that I was some lovesick puppy eager to do his bidding. Once I saw that it was Mack, I slipped my robe off. I strode to the door in my see-through lacy bra and barely there matching panties. All of the lights were still off and his silhouette seemed to encompass the whole entryway.

I opened the door. One large hand wrapped around the back of my neck and the other scooped me up in his arms. He kicked the door shut with the back of his boot. He carried me to the counter and roughly set me down. He pushed my legs apart and stood between them. His hard cock teased me through his denim.

"I've been waiting for this all day," he growled as he nibbled his way up my neck.

I angled my head to the side to give him all the access he needed. I moaned as his tongue soothed the sting of his teeth.

"Can't wait, baby."

He scooted my ass closer to the edge of the counter. He pulled at the lace of my underwear, tearing the material in two. His teeth grazed over my hardened nipples. The sheer material made it feel as though they were uncovered. He yanked down his pants as his mouth continued its feast on my breasts. My pussy tightened in anticipation when his cock nudged between my slick folds. He raised his mouth to mine. His tongue darted into my mouth the same time his cock plunged deep into my center. His tongue fucked my mouth in tandem with his cock. My pussy clenched around his dick as ecstasy ripped through me. He slammed into me one last time before his own release gripped him.

Mack kicked his jeans and boots off, scooting them across the floor. He picked me up effortlessly and made his way to the bedroom. He laid me on the bed as though I were a rare treasure. I smiled dopily from the euphoria of being fucked well. When the bed dipped from his weight, my grin grew. I wanted to feel him beside me and wake to him in the morning. I couldn't explain this new feeling but right in this moment, it felt right.

MACK 11

TRYING TO KEEP MY HANDS off Abbie was like leaving a Barbie doll in front of Riley and telling her not to play with it. No matter how hard I tried, my willpower wasn't strong enough. I watched her sleep in the early morning hours, soaking in her soft snores and sinful body. I burned her image into my mind. I would be out of pocket for the next week.

Forrest and I had set up our security business. Global Securities was finally up and operational. Between the two of us, we had scored a couple of easy jobs. Forrest took the two gigs close to town and I opted for the one in Tennessee. I wanted him to stay close to his family. I had no one here who needed my immediate attention, so I opted to take the weeklong job. An up-and-coming country singer wanted an extra body on her security team. Our company had been highly recommended. She had a two-day concert and some interviews that I would tag along to.

The business was in its early stages and we couldn't afford to deny too many jobs. Until the company was solvent, it was in our best interest to take as many gigs as we could fit between us. I had more money than I needed but that didn't mean I didn't care about making this partnership work. This would be a walk in the park compared to my last assignments. I liked country music, so it wouldn't be that much of a hardship for me. The only thing that sucked was that Abbie wouldn't be within arm's reach. She had me pussy-whipped. I wasn't in love with her but I sure as hell loved her pussy. The possibility of a future with her didn't scare me as much as I thought it would. However, right now we were enjoying each other.

She snuggled deeper into my chest. I ran my fingertips up and down her arm. With each pass of my fingers, she burrowed deeper. I rolled her on her back and trailed my lips along her delicate skin. Her nipples beaded the closer my mouth got. Tiny moans escaped her lush lips, driving all the blood in my body to my cock. Her body bucked when I took her sensitive peak into my mouth. Her nails bit into my scalp, sending a shock down my spine and straight to my dick. Even in her half-dream state, her body responded with fervor.

"Mack," she whispered huskily.

"Yeah, baby. I'm gonna make you feel good."

"Mmm, okay."

My mouth trailed down her belly. Her muscles quivered slightly with each pass of my tongue. I worked my way down to her mound. Fuck, she was soaking wet. Her pussy glistened, begging me to play. I pushed her knees up and opened her wide. Her sweet musk drove me mad. I darted my tongue between her folds and licked my way from her center to her clit. Her heels pressed into the mattress the minute I circled her clit. Her breaths came in short pants, shoving her pussy deeper into my mouth and I fucking loved it. My mouth ate every inch of her pussy like a starved man.

"Shit, Mack. I'm going to come."

"That's it, baby. I want to drown in your juices. Come

for me," I hummed against her pulsating clit.

Her inner muscles pulled at my fingers, sucking them in deeper. Her mouth lit with the raunchiest words as her orgasm tore through her body.

"Are you ready for me, baby?"

"God, yes. I need more."

I kissed up her body, leaving a trail of wetness in my wake. I placed my lips upon hers, stroking her tongue and letting her taste herself. My cock rested near her opening, demanding entrance. She wrapped her firm legs around my waist, digging her heels into my ass, and pushed me all the way in.

"You feel so good. I'm not going to last."

"Less talking and more action."

I chuckled and pumped faster and harder. I wanted to fuck her hard enough that she remembered that I had claimed her pussy. My mission was to ruin her for other men. I wanted her to only think of me when her pussy needed attention. My balls tightened when she screamed her release. I thrust in and out of her tight clench until I spilled my seed.

I rolled over and brought her backside to my chest. She felt amazing in my arms. Her body still glistened and her breathing had yet to calm down. I placed a kiss along her delicate neck. I could feel the steady beating of her heart beneath my lips. I didn't want to get up but I had a bag to pack and a boring drive ahead of me.

"Abbie?"

"Hmm," she purred.

"I've got to get going. I've stored my number in your phone. I'll be gone for a week. Try not to miss me too much."

She turned her head to the side and looked at me from the corner of her eye. "I should be back to tip-top shape by the time you get back. Call me when you get back to town and I'll see if I can fit you in my schedule." The corner of her mouth twitched. "Oh, and thank you for fixing my door."

I swatted her behind playfully. She squealed and I laughed. I placed a searing kiss against her delectable mouth. "My pleasure."

I walked into Forrest's office. "What's up, partner?"

"Not much. You ready for Nashville?"

"Just finished packing. I wanted to touch base with you before I headed out. Anything new that I need to know about before I hit the road?"

"Nothing really to it. Just keep her safe and in your sights. I'll be in and out of pocket. I've got those two conventions this week but nothing I can't handle. Boring stuff right now."

"Alrighty. I'll check in with you throughout the week. See ya later."

"Later."

I punched in Jenna Frost in Pandora. No better way to get acquainted with my client than to listen to the kind of music she put out. An hour in and I wished for earplugs. She was supposed to be the hottest new act out there. Must be with the tweens or whatever they are calling themselves these days. They were those kids who weren't old enough to drive themselves but had the attitude of a spoiled adult. I loved the good ol' country music, not this new wave-pop shit. It drove me nuts and made my skin crawl. I'd rather be tortured for three days straight than put up with this bullshit. Forrest didn't take the convention jobs because they were close to home. That fucker took them so he wouldn't be tempted to pop his eardrums. *Why couldn't I get Loretta Lynn?* That would've been an awesome gig. Her songs were hilarious and she was sassy. Had to love a woman who didn't mince words.

Jenna's music sounded like a mix between the Dixie Chicks and Taylor Swift. I will admit that I enjoyed some of their hits but not two concerts full of them. I rubbed my hand down my face. *This is what I left Abbie's bed for?* I prayed that she wasn't some airheaded bimbo. Not that I would have a whole lot of interaction with her. Most of my time would be spent with her normal security team and checking the venues. The only time I would be with her one-on-one was when she had her interviews. I was more of a contractor, lending my expertise to her normal security team.

I checked in to the hotel. Tomorrow I would meet with Jenna and her security detail. I would also comb through the venue and do a dry run of the route to her interviews. There was a shit ton to do. Tonight, the hours were mine. I like to have a clear head before a job but mine was filled with this morning's moans from my favorite redhead. I wanted to text her but I also didn't want to come off as some lovesick pussy.

I was the quintessential bad boy. I had been trained to kill and had the blood of many on my hands. I was proud of each and every one of them. Those kills were of those who were truly evil. I don't give a shit what those human rights activists claimed. Not all humans had the right to live. I made the choice to end a life when I pulled the trigger or used my bare hands. I never took those decisions lightly and I would get judged when my own time came. I would worry about that when I stood before the

Almighty.

I had signed on to protect the land of the free and all of its civilians. I had no regrets, only sorrow for my slain brothers I had lost along the way. There wasn't a day that went by that I didn't think of them. Serving alongside them had been my greatest pleasure. When my tours of duty were over and I was honorably discharged, I signed on to do the same kind of work but without the rules of engagement hanging over my head. I had lost too. Many of my brothers were killed before my eyes. I don't know why I worked for the outfit for as long as I did. Could be for retribution or maybe for the thrill. Call me an asshole but it paid the bills.

A restful night always seemed to be just out of reach. My wingspan was fairly long and yet it felt as though only my fingertips grazed the edges of my elusive dream state. I'm not complaining; my dreams harbored the death of my comrades. I wanted them to visit me but not in a mangled form. I longed to see them the way they were before the war and destruction had fucked us over.

I drove through the gated community. Each estate was immaculately kept. I wondered whether the grounds crew worked like secret ninjas at night so as to not disturb the homeowners. I've lived in an apartment most of my adult life, not really caring about yard work. Before that, it was the beautifully weed-filled Winding Lakes trailer park. My dad never stuck around long enough to give a shit about the aesthetics of our home. I did what I could for my mother but her attitude was much the same. The bottle meant more to her then a well-kept home. As soon as I was old enough, I joined the service and never looked back. Not even a small part of me felt guilty for that. She could rot in hell for all I cared.

I shook off the past like a mutt shaking its coat from the rain. I pulled onto the paved drive, stopping at the wrought-iron gate. I reached through my open window and pushed the button on the intercom system.

"Can I help you?"

"Mack Sinclair. Here to meet with Jenna Frost."

The gates opened and I drove through. I wondered whether she built this home or whether she bought it. Everything looked brand-new. The paint on the house didn't even look as though it had dried completely. *What the hell was one person supposed to do with all this space?* This seemed to be a huge waste of money. I'd rather have the land with a smaller home. A nice place where I could hunt, fish, and bury an intruder without questions. Not that I ever expected that but one needed to be prepared just in case.

I parked my truck right outside the front steps, not giving a shit about any protocol set in place. I climbed the decorative stone steps. I pounded my fist on the expansive oak door. I could've rung the doorbell but I couldn't find the fucker. The massive door crept open as though it were too heavy for the person on the other side.

A petite female stood in the entryway. Her hair curled around her face in perfectly styled blonde ringlets. Her oceanic eyes sparkled in conjunction with her mega-watt smile. I squinted behind my sunglasses.

"Hello, ma'am. My name is Mack Sinclair and I am here to see Jenna."

"Hi, Mack. I'm Jenna. It's nice to meet you." She held out her hand.

My hand engulfed her smaller one. "My pleasure."

I didn't think that it was possible but her smile widened as she scanned over my body. I winked, letting her know that I had caught her checking me out. I bet she left a lot of broken hearts in her wake. Too bad I don't mix business with pleasure. I learned that lesson the hard way. Plus, I was more than happy with Abbie for the moment.

"Please come in." She angled her body away from blocking the doorway but close enough that I would brush against her to pass.

I chuckled inwardly as my arm brushed her breasts.

Her heels clacked against the tile floor and echoed through the foyer. I looked up at the high ceilings and overpriced chandelier and realized that my entire apartment would fit in this room alone. She had incredible taste, albeit expensive. We exited the foyer and turned down the expansive hall. About a third of the way down, she opened up a door and led us into some kind of drawing room.

An unremarkable man stood to greet us.

"Mack Sinclair." I shook his outstretched hand.

"Dominick Braun, head of security."

"Please sit, gentlemen," Jenna stated with an air of authority.

I took a seat in one of the oversized leather chairs that faced the entryway and crossed my leg over my knee. I was curious as to what part I played. She had her own security detail; there wasn't a need for me. I could tell that Dominick liked to be in charge and would have a difficult time taking orders from me. I, unlike Dominick, preferred to stay in the shadows.

"All right, gentlemen. Are we done with the pissing match? I would like to get down to business."

I openly guffawed. She had pegged us both. We had been sizing each other up since we shook hands. From her outside appearance, I assumed that she would be a pushover; clearly she called the shots.

"There are certain holes in my security team that need to be patched. I called Mr. Sinclair because he is the best. He works in the shadows and gets results. Dominick, you are the head of the team and I am not pleased." She angled her youthful face toward me. "You come highly recommended. I want you to do whatever it is that you do and fix those holes."

Her eyes bore into Dominick, making him slouch in his chair.

She pointed her finger at Dominick. "There is a concert tonight and as you know, it's one of our biggest venues to date. The fans will be all over the place. I do not expect any surprises backstage. You got me?"

"Yes, ma'am."

"Good. One more fuck-up and you're through." She stood regally and strode to the door, making the rod up her ass look sexy. "Go brief the team and make sure they understand what's on the line tonight."

Dominick dashed through the door to do her bidding. She stood there with her hand still on the knob. Using her free hand, she rubbed her forehead. "I swear he wasn't this incompetent when I hired him."

She huffed out a frustrated sigh and slunk into one of the leather chairs. Her cool demeanor now gone, a weary persona took its place.

"He has gotten lazy. He is the head of your security team, correct?"

"Yes."

"He is already at the top, with no upward momentum. A guy like that needs motivation to do the job correctly. Making him aware that his place is expendable will motivate him in the right direction."

She raised her head. "Is that your professional opinion?"

A grin stole my previous blank expression. "You want my honest opinion?"

The twinkle in her eyes had come back and illuminated her stunning features.

"It's what I hired you for. No bullshit. Straight answers. Personal items have gone missing. My dressing room is littered with uninvited guests. I fear that things are only going to escalate and some crazed fan will get past my team."

"Look, Ms. Frost——"

"Jenna."

"Jenna. I'll stay in the shadows, watching your security detail, and report my findings at the end of the week. I will give them to you as brutally honest as you want."

"Thank you."

"My pleasure." I stood to leave. "Don't bother looking for me. I know your schedule and will be within arms reach the whole time."

"I'll walk you out."

"No need. I can find my way."

ABBIE 12

MY ASS CHEEK VIBRATED, MAKING me jump. I pulled out my phone and peered at the text that popped in.

ARE YOU STAYING OUT OF TROUBLE?

Nervous energy blasted through my body simply from looking at his message. I didn't want to feel needy and anxious. I wasn't that kind of girl. I was independent and didn't need a man to complete my life. I ran a successful business, had money in my bank account, and owned my home. I hung out with my friends when I pleased and loved not answering to anyone. Mack wasn't a typical guy. He had barged his way into my life. These feelings felt foreign to me. I wanted to see more of him and not only for a blow-your-mind orgasm. *No fucking way. Keep it casual, girl.*

NOT IF I CAN HELP IT.

THAT'S MY GIRL.

I bit the bottom of my lip. I wasn't his girl or anyone's girl, for that matter. No matter what emotions he pulled out of me.

I'M NOT YOUR GIRL.

YES YOU ARE.

He was delusional if he thought that I was his girl.

"Can I get a beer, sweetness?" one of the patrons called

from down the bar.

I put my phone back in my pocket and got back to work. Now was not the time to spend arguing a moot point. Serving my customers was my priority. Even if they could be annoying.

I blew out a breath as I strutted toward the obnoxious customer.

"I don't know, sugar––can you?" My voice oozed sugary sweetness with a hint of sass.

"May I get a drink, please?" His lips quirked and made the gesture more lecherous. "Gotta love a woman with a bite."

I leaned over the bar and invaded his personal space. I wanted to claw at his eyes and never make it possible for him to leer at a woman ever again. "What's your poison"––my voice dropped lower and dripped with venom as I glared daggers into his eyes––"sugar?"

His bloodshot eyes widened. The coloring of his iriss disappeared. "Umm––"

Hook, line, and sinker! "One draft beer coming up!" I sauntered away cheerily, pretty pleased with myself.

There is nothing better in the whole world than shutting down an asshole who thinks he is God's gift to women. Especially when that said asshole believes he has the right to speak to me, let alone any woman, that way. I hope, for his sake, that he got the message. He will get the house beer with extra foam because I can be a bitch like that. I deal with all kinds of customers. Some are what allow me to love my chosen career. Those who treat me as a piece of meat––or as subpar to them––buy more than alcohol from me. Owning and running a bar requires thick skin. I have layers upon layers that no patron will ever scratch. I can tolerate various drunken stages. What I cannot condone is disrespectfulness toward myself, my employees, or other patrons.

As the night wore on, I continued to stew over Mack's text. *Did I want to be his girl? Could I maintain a monogamous relationship?* All of these thoughts were unfamiliar to me. The longest relationship that I had was roughly two months long. Even at that, it was isolated to the bedroom. We never went out in public together or had an actual date. It never seemed necessary or the direction I had wanted to go with that guy. He was decent in bed and knew what I liked. So, I kept him around until we both went our separate ways.

I picked up my phone, wanting to find out more of what being *his* entailed. I started to text but then erased it. I began again and deleted it once more. This was beyond juvenile. I might as well grab a piece of paper and write: *will you be my boyfriend, check yes or no.* This is why I don't do relationships. At least when it was purely sex, there was no second-guessing or any real feelings involved. *Who wouldn't want everlasting love? But was that even a possible reality for me?*

My parents had that and look how it turned out. She was dead and he had pined for years for her until his own death. I was happy and sad that my parents had found that kind of love. For the nonbelievers, it was a testament that true love existed. For those of us who believed, but were more scared of mortality cutting it short, we might be better off indulging in shorter, less meaningful flings so that our hearts were only slightly broken instead of shattered at the end.

Ugh! I was disgusted with my frame of mind. I looked at the vintage clock on the wall. I willed the hands to move, merely seconds until last call. Finally the big hand struck and I flickered the lights. These last thirty minutes were going to be torturous.

I climbed the back stairs with a heavy heart and tired limbs. *Damn Mack for trying to define our relationship.* I walked toward the kitchen to pour myself a glass of water. I kicked my heels off before I entered the kitchen. My bare feet hit the floor and rejoiced in their freedom as I stepped barefoot on to the cold hardwood. I needed to rethink my choice of footwear for the bar but they made my legs look fantastic. The small light above the stove gave me enough light to find the correct cabinet for a glass.

I leaned against the sink, drinking the water, when cold chills traveled along my now hypersensitive skin. My body instantly froze in place. The glass stopped half-way between my mouth and the counter. I strained my ears, listening to every creak and moan from my home. Something was off but I couldn't put my finger on it. I felt it deep in my bones. I carefully put the half-full glass in the sink. I tiptoed to the front door. It was locked. I silently let out a breath that I had been holding in. I was scared but I also had to find out whether the rest of my home was safe. *Should I call someone?*

I pulled out my phone and hit Marie's number. I let it ring until her voicemail picked up. I hit the End button and redialed. *Damn it!* I didn't want to call Mack. I could handle this but I also didn't want my dead body stinking up the place if something were to happen. *Shit!* I hit the buttons on the screen, dialing his number. I didn't want him to answer and yet I was terrified he wouldn't.

"You miss me yet?" he answered in a deep tone.

"Mack," I whispered.

"What's wrong?" His voice instantly took on a commanding tone.

"I'm not sure. I haven't checked the rest of the apartment but something isn't right."

"Get out of there, now. I'll call Forrest to come and check it out."

I nodded my head in agreement but couldn't find my voice.

With a calmer and yet authoritative tone, he said, "Abbie, listen to me. Please, walk out your front door and get into your car and wait for Forrest. I'm going to hang up and I will call you right back."

"Okay."

I found some survival sense and silently stepped out of my home. Once my feet hit the pavement, I ran as fast as I could to my car. I jumped when my phone rang, dropping the phone in the process. I bent down and picked it up and swiped the screen.

"How are you doing, baby?"

His voice was softer this time, instantly making me feel safe.

"I'm better now. I'm sorry I interrupted you. I'm going to feel so stupid when Forrest gets here."

"Nothing to feel stupid for or sorry. I'm glad you called me. I'm sorry it's not me coming to check things out. He shouldn't be much longer. I'll feel much better once he goes through the place."

I sighed heavily and sunk into the seat. "Me too. Thank you." I shifted my hips to get more comfortable. "So tell me how the job is going."

"Nothing too spectacular. I'm pretty much just making sure that my client's security team is doing their job."

"So you are like a bodyguard?"

His deep chuckle sent goose bumps along my skin.

"More like private security. The client hired our company to come in and weed out any issues. Sometimes I will be required to be a bodyguard but not this time."

"Who is this mystery client?"

I was completely ignorant to his line of work.

"If I told you, I'd have to kill you."

"Really?" I was completely serious. Hell, one look at Mack and you'd come to the same conclusion.

His deep laughter was contagious and soon I was chuckling with him, even though it was at my expense.

"No, but it would violate client confidentiality. I'll tell you when I'm through with the job."

"Promises, promises."

I squeaked when someone knocked on my window-pane. I sucked in a breath and looked at the person.

"Abbie?"

"It's Forrest. He scared me for a minute. Hang on a sec."

I couldn't hear his response because I had put the phone in my lap. I rolled down the window.

"Hi, Forrest. Thank you for coming over. Let me hang up with Mack, and I'll go up with you."

"I've already gone through the house and it's all clear. If you want, I'll come up with you and stay until you are comfortable."

I held the phone back up to my ear. "Forrest is here and he says it's all clear. I'll call you back in a bit."

"Call me once you're settled."

"K, bye."

I hung up and really got a look at Forrest. He was almost as intimidating as Mack. He was about as tall and as muscular. His features were fierce but held a softness within that made you feel comfortable in his presence.

"You don't have to. I'll be fine. I feel so stupid for having you come over for nothing."

"Don't worry about it. I'll come up anyway just to make sure that everything is in its place. I need you to tell me if anything is missing."

The fear rushed back but I straightened my spine. "Good idea."

The walk back to my apartment was slow and tedious. A million thoughts ran through my mind the closer we got. Thankfully Forrest broke all of them apart.

"You are fine to enter. I only want you to make sure that all of your things are in their exact place. If it wasn't safe, I would not have let you back in."

With my hand on the doorknob, I twisted around to face Forrest. "Thank you. I don't know why I am being a baby. I'm not normally like this."

"It's scary thinking someone was in your home. Trust me, everything is good."

I nodded. *Why did I keep doing that?* Words were apparently hard for me to form. We walked in the apartment together. With each step, I felt marginally better. I looked throughout the apartment while Forrest stood, stoic, in the kitchen. I went through every room and found nothing amiss. I had double-checked my room and nothing. Yet, the creep factor was off the charts. I rubbed my arms, trying to ward off the chills.

"Does anything look disturbed?"

His voice echoed through the apartment.

I turned to go back into the kitchen where Forrest stood patiently.

"No. Is it weird that I still feel uneasy being here?"

"Not at all. I will change the locks on both doors in the morning. How about you come back home and stay the night with us?"

I wanted to be brave but I was too worked up. "Thanks, I think I will. Let me go grab a bag."

"I'll be out in the car."

Again, the nod was my go-to response.

Candice met us at the door when we arrived. Even at this late hour, she looked beautiful. Her blonde hair wasn't tousled in the least. Forrest took her in his arms and locked lips so fiercely I almost felt as though I were a voyeur. You'd think that he had been gone months instead of mere hours.

Candice pulled me into a motherly hug. I melted against her warmth, wishing mine were still around.

"Come on, honey. I've already made up your room. But first, come in the kitchen for a nice glass of whiskey."

I laughed. I can't remember any mother figure offering up whiskey. Maybe a glass of late-night tea or warm milk. A whiskey sounded wonderful right about now.

"You had me at whiskey." The smile that followed was small.

"I got a couple of calls to make. I'll come up to bed when I'm done. Goodnight, Abbie."

"Thanks again, Forrest. I appreciate your help."

It was his turn to nod.

I followed Candice and looked around. Their house was gorgeous. The kitchen was what dreams were made of. It was decorated with good taste and, most importantly, was inviting. I pulled out a chair and tucked my leg beneath me. I watched Candice pour two fingers' worth. She placed the glass in front of me and sat on the opposite side. I downed the drink in one smooth motion.

Her laughter punched some happiness through my morose thoughts. I grinned back.

"Thank you for putting me up for the night. I know you don't know me that well."

"It's no problem at all. I understand what you are going

through."

I glanced into her sympathetic eyes. Yes, she of all people would. Rumors were that her ex was a major physically abusive asshole. I had also heard that he had trashed her home at one point. What I was going through was minor compared to what she had to endure for years.

"You can stay here as long as you like. I know Mack would feel better if you stayed here until he returned home."

The sly smile didn't escape me.

"Thank you, again. I appreciate it." I sucked in a breath. "I feel so stupid. Forrest went through the apartment and he found nothing."

She placed her hand over mine. "Give yourself some credit. If your gut was telling you that things were off, then they were. Who are we to judge? For the record, I believe you. Forrest is thorough and even if he didn't find anything, it doesn't mean that your feelings were dismissed. It's better to be safe than sorry."

I smiled even though I didn't feel like it. She was right but some physical evidence would have made me feel justified with my current situation.

"Thank you. If you don't mind, I'm kind of tired."

"Come on, I'll show you to your room."

She led me through the expansive kitchen and up the ornate staircase.

"Your home is stunning."

"Thanks. The boys worked hard on restoring it to its former glory."

"The boys?"

"Forrest, Mack, Enzo, and Sal."

"Mack helped with all of this?" I swung my arms out with amazement. Not that he couldn't do this type of work; I just never would've imagined it.

"Don't sound so shocked. Mack is the iconic bad boy. Underneath all of that muscle and intimidation lies a heart of gold and master carpentry skills. He has come to mean a great deal to Riley and me. I'd hate for him to get hurt. You know what I mean?"

She opened the bedroom door for me to pass. I'm pretty certain that she didn't have to worry about me hurting him. Mack, on the other hand, had the potential to shatter my heart if I let him.

"Duly noted. Thanks again for opening up your home. I really appreciate it."

"Anytime. Get some rest. You'll need it before Riley wakes and knows you're here."

She chuckled and shut the door, leaving me in silence. I stripped to my underwear and climbed into bed. I snuggled into the comforter and then grabbed my phone to text Mack. I should call him but I didn't want to talk anymore tonight.

STAYING WITH CANDICE AND FORREST. NOTHING FOUND AT THE APARTMENT. I AM SAFE. THANK YOU FOR CALLING FORREST FOR ME. I'LL TALK TO YOU LATER.

His response was immediate.

ANYTHING FOR MY GIRL, GLAD YOU ARE SAFE AND SOUND. TALK TO YOU SOON.

MACK 13

"WE DON'T KNOW WHO THE hell this guy is. We need to keep an eye on her. Can you handle the caseload for the short-term? I'll help if they are close to home."

"No problem. I can handle the business side of things. Abbie's safety is more important right now."

I could hear the static from the phone shifting around. Before I could ask what he was doing, he started talking again.

"Just so you know, I didn't show her what that sick fuck left in the apartment."

"Why the fuck not? She needs to be aware of the situation."

"Because she wasn't in the right state of mind."

"Damn it. I'm going to have to tell her over the phone. Forrest, you really fucked this one up. This is not a conversation that should take place on the phone," I shouted.

"All right, calm down. I will tell her tomorrow. Candice will be there to help comfort her. I figured the less she knew, the better. I see your point, though. She should be informed and actively trying to figure out who this could be."

"Forget it. I'm coming home tonight. Make sure she stays away from the apartment until she goes into work.

Let her borrow something to wear from Candice. I'll tell her tonight after her shift."

"The job's not done and I'm around to keep an eye on her. I'm leaving to put the new locks on the doors first thing in the morning. She can follow me home. I'll keep an eye on her until you get there. Make sure it's when the job is finished, not any sooner."

Damn if that didn't sound like a fucking order.

"I've already got what I need to finish this up. I'll be home tomorrow evening. One more thing. I am your partner, not your subordinate."

"Shit, Mack. That's not what I meant. I just didn't want you to fly off the handle when I can take care of this while you finish up. If you checked yourself, you wouldn't have even considered that a thought."

"Gotcha, boss."

"Fuck you. Get your shit together and come protect your girl."

I chuckled, feeling better knowing that Forrest and I were back on good terms. I was pissed when I had made that comment. Sometimes diarrhea squirts out of my mouth when I don't think things through.

The audience erupted into deafening screams the minute Jenna walked on stage. The crowd consisted of individuals of all ages. I assumed that her popularity was more for teeny-boppers. A vast number of women and men were closer to my age. Jenna addressed the crowd and they rose to their feet, going wild. Her stage presence electrified the crowd with every note she sang.

I stood backstage, entranced in her version of "The

Door Is Always Open" by Waylon Jennings. Other artists have covered this song and the only one that I liked besides Waylon's was Jamey Johnson's and now Jenna's. Not sure whether she had recorded this on her album but I totally would purchase it from iTunes. In the span of three minutes, she had converted me into a Frost fan. My body swayed to the music and my lips moved with the lyrics. Our voices blended with Jenna's and had become one. At this moment, I was as smitten with her as the rest of the crowd. When the crowd burst into applause, I snapped out of my trance. *Well I'll be damned, that woman had a damn good voice.* It wasn't a pop song or even one that many would know. It had to be on an album; there was no way in hell that over half of the stadium knew that song.

I stayed in street clothes intentionally. Only Dominick had seen me personally and yet not long enough for him to pick me out of a crowd. While I hid in the shadows, I watched money exchange hands between fans and Dominick as well as other security members. Once the money was exchanged, a member of the security team would walk into the dressing room and exit a few minutes later. I followed each person who had exchanged money with Dominick or another team member. When I was clear of any team member's sight, I stopped the individual, scaring them enough to give me the items that had been taken. Some of the people had handed them their phones for pictures. Which I promptly deleted. Others had small mementos, such as single flowers from her bouquets, toiletries, and other tokens. It wasn't hard to shake them up. They already had a guilty conscience. It only took minor probing to get them to give me what I wanted.

I personally wanted to maim and destroy every guy who I had discovered was dirty. I didn't give a shit about their reasons, only that they went against every fiber of my being. The funny part was that Dominick knew about my presence but thought himself too slick to be caught. *What an arrogant fuck.* Considering Forrest wasn't here to help with damage control and the necessity to protect Abbie, I made sure those urges were quickly snuffed out.

When the crowd began to chant "Encore!" I slipped past Dominick and entered her dressing room. The look on his face was priceless. He hadn't expected me to be here tonight, let alone without his knowledge. I pulled out my miniature notepad and began to write my observations. I sunk deeper into the comfy couch cushions while I waited. The door flung open and a whirlwind of a breathless and glistening Jenna flew through the door. I remained seated in silence as she fluttered about the large room.

Mere minutes went by before she hurled herself onto the opposite side of the couch. She adjusted her body until she finally found a comfortable position.

"Okay, Mack. Spill your findings. I didn't expect you so early. I figured it would take more time."

I couldn't help but chuckle. "Sweetheart, I only needed five minutes and I had it all figured out."

She cocked her head to the side, stunned. "Really? Enlighten me then."

"First, I've got to compliment you. You are a fabulous singer. You command the stage like no one I've seen in years. I loved your version of *'The Door Is Always Open.'*"

I sounded like a complete schmuck.

A genuine smile took over her features, showcasing her playful nature.

"My, my, Mack. You're going to make me blush."

I burst out laughing, knowing full well Jenna Frost

never blushed. "Let's put your ego back in check and get down to business."

"And there is the Mack who has come to grow on me."

I handed over the small slip of paper. "These are the names of your security team who are loyal and have your best interests at hand. Anyone not on this list should be fired immediately and reported. That, of course, is my opinion. I texted you the pictures of what I caught those employees doing."

"Dominick's name isn't on this list. Why am I not surprised?"

"Because you already knew that he allowed fans access to some extent. He exchanges money and gives them items from your dressing room that belong to you." I took the once-empty trash bin and had filled it with all of the items that were taken from this evening. I slid it over. "I acquired all of the belongings that I could. I don't know if that is everything. At one point, I was engrossed in your show and I admit that I wasn't paying a lick of attention to your team."

It wasn't a proud moment but I wasn't ashamed of it either. That was a damn good song. Any moron with good musical taste would've done the same thing.

"That's a lot of items to have been missing. Some of these I would chalk up to misplacing." She held up her lipstick tube as an example. "I can't believe I've let this go on this long. I've known for quite a while that something was up. I just didn't expect Dominick to be a part of this."

"You are busy and scattered on these nights. It's easy to overlook what is going on with the team that you hired to protect you and your belongings. You pay them to do a job and that's what they are supposed to do. They watch you, not the other way around."

For someone so put together, she looked lost.

"Jenna, trust me, I know what you are going through. It's a violation of your trust and your personal space. I've got a couple of names that I'll send you. Call them. I know for a fact that they would love to come work for you. I used to work with them and they are looking for something different. You won't have to worry about loyalty with them."

She looked up at me, seemingly recharged.

"I know that our contract continues through the end of the week but I have some things that have come up back home that I have to take care of. If you give those guys a call, they can be here within the next twenty-four hours and will pick up from where Dominick and the others left."

Finding a reputable security team that you could trust didn't happen overnight. *Who knew how long Dominick's fingers reached in this town?* I didn't want another douche to take his place. I wanted the best for her and if she did what I told her to, she would get the best.

I stood. There was no reason to prolong this visit. She had the pertinent information. I was no longer needed. "Would you like me there when you talk to Dominick and the rest of the guys?"

"No, it's not necessary. I'll tell them once the new team gets here and they can help me throw them out on their asses!"

"That a girl! Now, come on. I'll take you home."

The ride to her house was quiet and peaceful. I felt as though I did a thorough enough job even though I had cut it extremely short.

We pulled up to her house. Before she exited the car, she turned toward me. "Thanks for the ride. If you are ever in town, give me a buzz or if you're ever in need of some concert tickets."

"You got it. Keep in touch, kid."

She had a good head on her shoulders and she was sassy as shit. *Abbie and she would make good friends.* I drove off, grabbed my shit from the hotel room, and headed home.

The five hours that it took to get home moved at a turtle's pace. I swear, traveling with only the radio and the stars to keep you company was like a baby's lullaby. My eyelids were heavy by the time I parked behind the Hickey. The sunlight had barely peeked over the horizon. Before I got out of the car, I texted Abbie.

UNLOCK YOUR DOOR, GORGEOUS. I WANT TO SLEEP NEXT TO YOU.

A couple of minutes went by without any response. She was probably sleeping and wouldn't hear the phone. I was going to have to pound on her door again. I got out of the car and trudged up the steps. As I got to the door, ready to start pounding, her text came through.

IT'S OPEN.

Thank God. I didn't want to have to replace another door. I opened it up and walked right through the kitchen. I opened up her bedroom door and stood there admiring her cute frame curled in a fetal position with the covers covering every aspect of her womanly body except for her serene face.

I walked silently to the other side of the bed and quickly undressed. I slid under the covers and gathered my treasure to my chest. I inhaled her sultry perfume and burrowed myself as close to her as I could get. A soft sigh escaped her luscious lips as I drifted off into a dreamless sleep.

I woke to a sea of electrical currents rolling through my body. My skin pulled tight against my constricted muscles. My heart raced inside my chest. Her warm mouth swallowed my morning hard-on as though its very essence would seal her soul to mine. The fogginess of sleep continued to abate the more she worked me with her mouth.

"Somebody missed me." I chuckled.

She grazed her teeth along my length, meant to warn but it had the opposite effect. Instinctively, I drove my cock deeper into her throat.

She licked the base of my cock. "I only missed your dick. Don't mix the two."

Ouch. The smile that formed from my lips didn't wane. She could lie to herself all day and I'd still know the truth. It was the way she looked at me as though she craved my touch. It was the way her breath hitched when I came near her. Her voice instinctively dropped an octave every time she spoke to me. No, her body never lied.

I placed my finger under her chin. "Get up here."

Her animalistic grin made me want to ravage her delectable mouth. I traced the outline of her lips with my tongue. She opened for me, and I plunged inside, hungrily taking possession. She broke the kiss and straddled my hips. Her skilled fingers arranged my throbbing cock between her warm folds. Her head fell back as she moved her hips forward and back. Each time the head of my cock rubbed against her clit, she moaned in ecstasy. I reached up and twirled both nipples between my fingers. Her movements picked up speed the closer her orgasm came.

"That's it, baby. Use my cock to come. You're so fucking hot," I growled.

"Oh, shit. Mack, I'm going to come," she screamed.

"I'm right there with you."

Her body tightened when her orgasm ripped through her. It was so fucking hot that I couldn't hold back. I reached behind her and gripped both ass cheeks as I followed suit. She did all the work and I was breathing as though I had run a marathon with my field pack on. Death by Abbie's pussy was the only way I wanted to go. I kissed her one last time before she slid off my body.

"That's a homecoming I could get used to." I chuckled as I got out of bed to get cleaned up.

In all my naked glory, I stood on the side she lay sprawled out on. "You hungry?"

Her sweet chuckle speared through my heart. She had me wrapped and didn't even know it.

"Yes, starving."

I cleared the plates from breakfast. I wanted to get this talk over with her quickly and decide the best course of action. I looked over at her sweet presence and almost lost my nerve. Scaring her was the last thing that I wanted to do. She had to know the severity of the situation that she was in. So I figuratively pulled on my big boy pants, grabbed some nerves, and sat next to her. I pulled her legs onto my lap and began to massage her feet. I wanted to soften the blow and yet I simply enjoyed touching her.

"Forrest wasn't exactly honest with you when he said that he didn't find anything in your apartment."

"What do you mean, he wasn't exactly honest?"

Her muscles constricted underneath her skin. I continued to massage her feet and ankles.

"There was a pair of panties lying on your bed, full of semen, and another pair torn to shreds."

Her breath hitched and still I continued.

"Forrest put them in a plastic bag and took them to a detective I know at the precinct." Before she could withdraw into herself, I wanted to fish around to see whether she might know who had left those for her to find. "Do you know who would leave you something like that?"

She shook her head ferociously. "No. I can't think of anyone who would even have access to my home. The only key that I have ever given out was to my friend Marie. She would never give anyone a copy."

"Okay. Maybe the detective will get a hit on the DNA. Let's forget about this for a moment. I'll stay here with you until we figure out who is behind this."

"Oh, no you won't. I will not let some punk scare me. This is my life and I am not running from it."

"At least let me stay with you so that I can be here if anything happens. I'll sleep on the couch."

She stood and started to pace the kitchen. She whipped back around to face me. Her fiery hair flowed as though they were hot embers released from an uncontrollable forest fire. Determination set deeply in her gorgeous green eyes. I admired the hell out of her. She owned the situation and would not let some douchebag throw her into a fearsome life. The need to protect her was strong and I would. Simply because she wouldn't let me stay with her didn't mean that I wouldn't be around. I was called a ghost for a reason.

"No. I can protect myself. I don't need you to be my knight in shining armor. Don't take that the wrong way. I am grateful for the help that you have given me already. This is my fight, not yours. I can't let you come in here and take over my life. What if this guy is never caught? Are you going to give everything up just to stick by my side?"

I grinned evilly on the inside. *You bet your sweet ass I'd give up everything. I wouldn't even think twice about it.*

"You are an independent woman. I get that. That doesn't mean that I can't be here to help when you need it." I got up and took her hands in mine. "I want you safe for purely selfish reasons." I grinned as I raised her delicate hands to my lips. I wanted to cherish this woman forever. Call me a pussy for thinking that way but it was the truth. "How about a compromise?"

I kissed the inside of her palms, working my way up the inside of her wrists.

"And that would be?"

She was softening and I fucking loved it.

"I'll stay here until this guy is caught and then I'll go back to my apartment and let you have your space."

She cocked her head to the side while she thought of my plan. There was no compromising; it was what I had initially offered. I wasn't backing down.

"All right. That sounds fair. Only until this guy is caught."

I was jumping up and down on the inside, throwing around imaginary high fives. She so wants me. *Yep, totally a thirteen-year old trapped in a middle-aged body.* I picked her up and laid her out on top of the kitchen table. I inched her shorts over her hips, down her long legs, and straight to the floor. Gloriously naked from her hips down, she lay for my taking. I loved her with my mouth until she screamed my name and then again until her whole body shook with the intensity of her orgasms. She would soon see how beneficial this arrangement could be.

Being with her day and night would be the easy part. The hard part was catching that fucker and not killing him in front of her. I wouldn't accept any part of her becoming broken from some sadistic fuck who got off on evoking fear in others, especially with the ones I loved.

ABBIE 14

"GIRL, I THINK HE IS trying to kill me."
"Death by orgasm! Come on––who doesn't want to go out that way!" Marie screeched.

I sat, cocooned in her favorite throw, and slowly sipped my coffee, silently agreeing with her.

"Why is he moving in with you again? I mean, you have never let a guy stay over for more than a night. You must l-o-v-e him." She cackled at her own hilarity.

"This is only temporary." I rolled my eyes.

"So what gives? Are you going to make me guess all the reasons? Because I could be here all day, trying to figure out your crazy mind."

I sighed heavily. I had to tell her about my stalker but I didn't want her flipping out. It was the right thing to do. She was my best friend in the entire world and the only family I had left. She deserved to know what was going on in my life. If the roles were reversed, I would be pissed that she had left me in the dark.

"I have a stalker."

"You have a what?"

"A stalker."

"No shit. Is he hot? I always wanted one of those!" She fanned herself.

"I'm being serious. He jacked off into a pair of my

panties and left them on my bed." I looked down into my coffee, trying to find the answers. None came to the surface.

"Are you shitting me?"

I continued to gaze into my coffee. "I wish I were." I looked up into her surprised-filled eyes. "That's why Mack is staying with me. At least until this guy is caught."

She pulled me into her arms like a mother would and stroked my hair. "It's going to be all right. Mack will protect you and the guys at the bar will look out for you as well. It's safer that he stays with you. I know that you aren't comfortable with him there but it won't be for long. Mack looks like a mean son-of-a-bitch who will go to great lengths to keep you safe."

She tipped my chin up with her fingers. "I'd ask you to stay with me but I know that you won't take me up on the offer." She chuckled and then became serious again. "Promise me that you'll stay safe? This is serious, Abbie."

I nodded. "Thanks, girl, but I don't want to put you or any of your family in danger. I know it is. I promise but I'm not going to hide behind Mack."

"No one is asking you to. Just because he is helping you doesn't mean that you are helpless. You don't have to give up your life to have a relationship with him, either. You can have both."

I stayed silent. I wasn't sure I believed that. Mack would be easy to love. He was selfless and cared for those around him. Oh, he was dark but with a lot of light mixed in too. I didn't know whether we would work. Giving up my independence was something that was non-negotiable. Marie seemed to think I wouldn't have to do that. I only needed to focus on one day at a time. Looking too far in to the future gave me the heebie-jeebies.

"Do you have any idea who it might be?"

Marie's question brought me back in to focus.

"I honestly don't know. You're the only one who had a key, which reminds me—I need to give you a copy of the new one. Forrest changed the locks. No one stands out in my mind."

"I'm going to go make us some more coffee while we think this through. Two heads are better than one."

The couch cushions enveloped my defeated body. A pain began at the base of my temples. I continued to rack my brain and still came up empty-handed. Not one guy stood out in my mind. The more I thought about it, the more my headache pounded.

"I've got to run to Sam's later. You want to go with me?"

Her question triggered something but it was just out of reach. It niggled at the back recesses of my mind. *Fuck it!* I was going to drive myself crazy if I didn't let it go for a while.

"Yeah, sure," I hollered back.

I sent a quick text to Mack to let him know I wouldn't be back until later. There was no sense in making him worry.

HANGING OUT WITH MARIE. BE HOME LATER.

As usual, his response was immediate. **BE CAREFUL. SEE YOU WHEN YOU GET HOME.**

Looking down at the text made my body tingle with warmth and excitement. There were definitely perks to living with Mack. He was lethal in the bedroom. It took him no time at all to find my erogenous buttons, as well as some that I hadn't known existed. Describing Mack was exceptionally hard for me. He was so much more than hot and good in the sack. Every time I was near him, it felt as though his soul reached for mine. I couldn't help but be drawn to him. I had no control over my mind or body when he was in the same room.

"What about the needle-dick guy?" she hollered from the kitchen.

I totally forgot about him. He was the most recent guy I had taken home. He gave off creepy vibes but he didn't strike me as the violent type. More like a typical, horny, college boy. She handed me a fresh cup of steaming coffee.

"Nah. He doesn't seem that ambitious."

"Hmm. I've run out of ideas. You've gone through a dry spell lately. Before him, it was Gage, off and on."

"That's the thing that doesn't make sense. Why is it happening now? Is it one of my patrons, some random guy in a store I said hello to, or a guy I slept with?" I threw my hands up in the air, completely frustrated.

"Girl, I just don't fucking know." She smacked the cushion with finality. "Let's get out of here and go get some pizza. Fuck going to the store and fuck stalkers."

I giggled because she was right. Fuck it. I couldn't control what this person would do or if it would ever happen again. What I could control was how I reacted to this whole situation. I would not waste another minute trying to figure out the pointless. *It is what it is.*

I wasn't even remotely hungry but I would absolutely throw down some Dispenza's pizza. "I'm in."

As soon as we walked through the door and the delicious aroma hit our nostrils, my stomach growled. My hand automatically covered my belly in attempt to quiet its rumbling.

"Tracy's on a quick break. You girls go ahead and seat

yourselves," Roselva called from the kitchen.

We headed to one of the back booths. I crossed my leg underneath my other one. I liked sitting at a booth. They were more comfortable than the chairs. I could hear Rose pounding her feet against the linoleum as she came near. She set our usual sodas on the table in front of us.

"You girls want the usual?" Her loud voice carried farther than our table.

Italians were a boisterous bunch, or so she claimed. Although, Marie and her family were a loud bunch when they all got together.

We both answered. "Yes, ma'am."

Her searing gaze turned in my direction. "Madone, child, you look like you've been worked hard and put away wet. What's got you troubled, child?"

How on God's green Earth does she do that? I wondered whether she had a crystal ball hiding behind the pasta bins.

"Nothing your magical pizza slice can't cure."

She winked. "Your medicine will be out shortly." With one last intense look, she turned and headed back to the kitchen.

"I swear, Marie, that she might be psychic," I whispered. If I had spoken any louder, she would have heard my remark.

Marie tossed her head back with laughter. "She's probably brewing a few spells as we speak."

"There may be a potion in the pizza sauce that gives her a direct link into our thoughts!"

Roselva came back to the table and deposited our pie. The steam wafted off the top, sending the smell of garlic straight to my gut. Saliva pooled into my mouth.

"The magic is in the dough, not the sauce." She clicked the heels of her orthopedic shoes and cackled all the way back to the kitchen.

The two of us stared, dumbfounded, at each other. Then we both busted out laughing. Marie and this pizza parlor were exactly what my soul needed. I already felt a million times better.

I said good-bye to Marie and headed home. I trotted up the stairs, excited to hand over some of the pizza slices that I saved for Mack. If I ate any more, I wouldn't be able to work in anything other than my yoga pants. It was a weekday and the bar wouldn't draw much of a crowd, so yoga pants it was and another slice in my belly.

I flung open the door and called out, "Mack, you gotta try this pizza. You'll never find another slice as good. It will ruin you forever."

Silence greeted me back. I set the box on the counter, where a slip of paper rested.

HAD TO GO INTO WORK FOR A BIT. I'LL SEE YOU LATER.

I shrugged, slightly disappointed that he wasn't here. I popped in my earbuds and blasted some Blues Traveler. I grabbed the vacuum from the closet and set about cleaning up the place. I loathed cleaning but I also couldn't have Mack thinking that I lived in filth. I usually gave the apartment a thorough cleaning when I took a mini vacation from the bar. I was the only one living here, so it wouldn't take that long. Cleaning, in a way, was cathartic. It was mind-numbing work and I was pleased with the way the place sparkled when I was finished. I

put away all of my supplies and went to get ready for
work.

MACK 15

"IT'S TIME TO DRAW THIS fucker out," I seethed.

"And your proposed plan is to do what exactly?"

Short of an eye roll, Forrest was merely playing along, pacifying me.

"Stick to her like glue. Wherever she goes, I go."

"That's your brilliant plan? Really?"

I huffed. "Yeah. There is no better way to draw him out by making him think that we are together."

He cackled in my face. "You sound just as delusional as her stalker. We will wait for his next move. Our chances increase exponentially if we sit back. He will do something stupid and we will be there when he does."

"How in the world do you even consider waiting a better plan?" I banged my fists against his mahogany desk.

His calendar flipped up in the air and landed on the floor. He never batted an eye at my sudden outburst. Simply picked up the calendar and placed it in its previous spot.

"If you'd get your head out of Abbie's ass, you'd realize that we have nothing to go on except for a pair of semen-filled panties. The DNA turned up absolutely zilch. We don't know anything at this point. Don't go all gorilla mode and scaring the fucker off before we can get a solid lead."

Goddamn him and his level-headedness. He had the same fierce patience when he formulated his plan to snuff out Candice's ex-husband. I was with him every step of the way and he never lost his focus. Sometimes I wanted to hate him. I tried viciously to dredge up that particular emotion and damn it, only love for my brother surfaced. I ran my hand over my face. *What a fucking mess.* I itched for a target or a hint of one so that I could go hunting. Unfortunately, I would have to sit on my fucking haunches until the opportunity presented itself. Before I met Abbie, I could go days in the desert or mountains and wait until the right conditions existed to carry out my mission. Now that she was the target, it was all I could do to sit back and wait for something to happen

"Mack, you need to listen to me on this one. I know what you are going through. I've been in your exact position. We will get this guy but you are going to have to chill the fuck out. I know Abbie means a lot to you and we will keep her safe. I promise you, brother, she will not be harmed." He swiveled his chair to grab the folder behind him. "I want you to take a look at these guys. Their resumes are all in there. I personally know two of them and the other two come highly recommended from the field. Let me know what your thoughts are and if you agree, we will get them on board. We need more manpower."

I grabbed the file. "I'll look them over. Are you planning on putting any of the new hires on Abbie's tail?"

"I thought about having two of them shadow her. You can't be with her every waking minute. I need you here too. The prick will never try anything if you are always there. He is going to want to get her alone and he can't do that if you are living with her and dangling from her arm all the time."

Damn, I really hated when he was right. Since Abbie came into my life, I haven't had the ability or the desire to be rational. Truth be told, it had been since I reunited with Forrest. I had become jaded in every aspect of my life. I had spent too many years spilling blood and alienating myself from the world. It wasn't the Army or the war that had jaded me. No, the Army had given me life and a purpose. I had brothers and sisters to protect, to keep them safe, and to bring them back home to their families. After my third tour was over, I had become burned out and in desperate need of something different.

Forrest had introduced me to the outfit so I could continue doing what I loved without the restrictions of the government. The outfit was comprised of a small group of billionaires with a vigilante mindset. They had hired about ten of us with similar backgrounds. We all had military training, no families, and the desire to rid the planet of the vilest individuals known to man. I had enjoyed my job, every minute of it. My kills would no longer prey on the innocent and I was proud of that. But somewhere along the line, my life had become hollow.

The man sitting directly across from me had helped me to find a true life again and rid most of the darkness that had started to seep into my heart. He gave me the most valuable gift: a family. I had never really had one and didn't realize how much I wanted one. Now, I had the sweet giggles of my goddaughter Riley, Candice's sisterly love, and hopefully Abbie's love. My desire to create a family of my own had hit me harder than I had thought possible. I knew it in my soul that Abbie was the only woman for me. My love for her drove my need to protect her to scrambling heights. Which, in turn, generated chaos in my thought process.

"If you keep squeezing that folder with your meaty

paws, those files will be useless."

I hadn't realized that I had a death grip on them. I loosened my hold and stood. "I'll look these over and let you know my thoughts before I head to the bar to meet Abbie."

"Sounds good. We have some prospects in the works that could bring our business to a whole new level. I want to get these guys hired ASAP."

I nodded and headed toward my office. I sat down and propped my feet on the desk. I opened the file while thinking about what a shitty partner I've been. Forrest had been carrying my weight ever since I drove into town. It was time to be the person that he believed he could count on.

Landon was barely out of his twenties, with a baby face. He had a hard edge hidden beneath his innocent looks. His background was impressive. Then again, didn't we all have impressive skills? I hadn't worked with him from the outfit but that didn't necessarily mean he had worked for them. Those of us employed by them were generally kept separate from one another. It was probably easier to pick us off if we decided to defect from the company.

Knox was a thick motherfucker. I didn't have to even read his file. He had partnered with Forrest and he was one bad dude. He was the type to slam your face into his fist and then ask questions later. A fiercely loyal bastard to the person he was guarding. He would be a great addition to the team and to keep watch over Abbie when I couldn't. He had my vote.

From looking over Holt's file he was a certifiable nut. He had made it his mission in life to become captured as often as he could. It was brazen and deranged. It's no wonder that his nickname was Houdini. He escaped every compound and prison that contained him and in return brought home hundreds of imprisoned civilians and military personnel. It looked as if he went underground for two years. Nobody had heard from him in that time. I had always thought of him as a myth but here he was, in black and white. I wondered how Forrest had found him. So far, three out of three had my glowing recommendations.

Shep, the fourth candidate, was a complete mystery to me. On paper, he had all the right credentials. On all accounts, a fascinating background. Something didn't gel right. I couldn't figure out what it was. I took all the resumes and headed to Forrest's office.

"I agree to three of them. I want Knox and Holt to shadow Abbie. I got a good feeling about them. I agree to hire Landon. He would make a great addition but I am unsure of Shep. I feel as though I am missing something with him."

Forrest chuckled. "And you'd be correct. Shep is the master of deception. He hides in plain sight. He gives off that sticky vibe in person and yet you can't help but like him. He will be our golden goose. As a matter of fact, I've known him and Knox for years."

I looked over at him, completely aghast. "I find it hard to believe that you would be in cahoots with Shep. He doesn't seem all that law-abiding. More like prison material."

He laughed even harder. "He has never spent time in prison and neither have we. Mack, you know that we both belong behind bars for what we did to Eugene and that's not counting what we have done in the past. Since when did you become all high and law-abiding?"

"Shut up. You know what I mean. I got a bad feeling about him."

"How about we hire him for a trial period and if he

doesn't work out, no harm in sending him on his way?"

"This is why you are the brains of the operation."

"What are you, the beauty?"

We both cracked up with that. I was far from poster boy material. "Nope, just the brawn."

On the ride home, I thought a lot about Shep. I still couldn't put my finger on any solid intel that deterred me from hiring him. I had to trust Forrest's instincts and his knowledge of the man. I hope he didn't prove us wrong and make our lives a logistical nightmare.

I took the stairs two at a time. I almost blew through the kitchen door when a small package caught my attention from the corner of my eye. I picked it up and set it on the table. I looked for a return address or some kind of note. It was completely void of any kind of markings. It was odd that it wasn't even addressed to her. Maybe she was expecting it. I left it on the table in plain sight so she would see it later. I took a quick shower before I headed to the bar, putting everything out of my mind except for seeing my girl.

It was early yet and the place was packed to the gills. Through the weekdays, it was mainly me and occasionally Eddy. It didn't take me long to see that they were falling behind. In the background, I could hear a deep, bluesy voice, singing about his baby being gone. I looked over the standing crowd and realized that it wasn't Broken Down playing but Mason. Mason was the bar-back on the weekends. His voice was rich and soulful. His hook-up book would be filled tonight. My gaze caught Abbie, and I grinned devilishly at her. She was a genius to bring him on during the week to drum up business.

I stalked behind the bar and grabbed my girl. I planted a searing kiss on her ruby-painted lips. I could hear cat-calls around the bar. I chuckled before I let her go.

"Put me to work. Where do you need me the most?"

"Out on the floor. The ladies are going to go bat-shit crazy between you waiting on them and Mason caressing them with his sultry voice."

I tapped her behind, rolled up my sleeves, and went to do her bidding.

Holy shit! These women were crude and horny. Hell, some of them looked as though they were going to slide right out of their chairs. I lost count on how many times my ass was grabbed.

I wrapped my arm around Abbie's waist and whispered in her ear. "You owe me. These women are like vultures."

"Hmm. I'll think of something to make you feel even more dirty."

I nipped at her ear. "Damn right, you will."

The drinks continued to pour well past his set. He sat at a corner table, eating up the attention. I silently cheered him on. Finally, Abbie flicked the lights. I don't know how she worked like this all the time. It had been exhilarating but I was spent. My feet hurt and my back ached. All I wanted to do was take my girl upstairs and wash away the cheap perfume and grabby hands. It was entertaining and boosted my confidence in the beginning but after a couple of hours they started to grate on my nerves. I wasn't cut out to be the piece of meat hanging on the hook. I openly laughed. *What was I thinking?* I was a man and I had loved every minute of the attention and now my girl would benefit from my hyped-up ego.

"What's so funny?"

"Not a thing." I continued to chuckle.

Mark that down as the fastest time on record for cleaning up. I tossed the mop in the empty bucket and rolled it into the supply closet. She locked the door and I swiftly hauled her over my shoulder and climbed the stairs. She was all mine. Her husky giggles spurred my legs to move like the Road Runner fleeing Wile E. Coyote. I tossed her on the bed and began haphazardly removing her clothing. I gazed upon her gloriously naked body. I took my fill as she lay there breathing heavily. She had been masterfully created, only for me.

I wanted to take my time with her but the way her green eyes devoured me made me lose my remaining control. I shucked my clothes and climbed the bed. She gasped as her budded nipples brushed against my bare chest. My dick throbbed with urgency as her silky skin mingled with mine. My hand caressed her thigh as my mouth swooped down and melded with hers. I raised my mouth from hers and gazed into her smoldering eyes. She had my insides all twisted.

"Mack," she pleaded.

I recaptured her lips, swallowing her last words. With each kiss, I demanded more. My fingers danced along her spine. Her body shivered beneath every stroke. I explored every inch of her soft flesh with the tips of my fingers as I kissed a path down her slender neck, to her chest, until I reached the swell of her breasts. I licked each swell before I moved my tongue over the taut bud. I languidly swirled my tongue around her small pink globe until it turned marble hard. She withered and moaned from the onslaught. My hand replaced my mouth so I could pay equal attention to the other hardened peak.

Her fingernails dug into the skin of my back as I slid my hand down her stomach and between the apexes of her thighs. She instantly opened for me. My sweet Ruby knew exactly what she wanted. The tips of my fingers slid between her wet folds. My greedy fingers breeched her opening and thrust deep into her warm center. Her heels dug into the mattress as she pushed her hips up. She took what she wanted while I watched with rapt fascination. I wanted to be buried deep inside but I held back, enjoying the way her body moved beneath me. I circled her clit with my thumb while my fingers drove in and out of her. Her breathing increased as she chased her orgasm. Her inner muscles began to tighten. I pulled my fingers away.

 Beneath her heavy lids, her eyes sharpened, throwing daggers in my direction. I swiftly replaced my fingers with my greedy cock. Her eyes once again glazed over. Her sweet sigh made my balls tighten and my cock swell even more. My thrusts quickened as her muscles gripped my cock. My restraint quickly dissolved. Her inner muscles milked my cock and her moans grew louder. Her nails dug deeper the closer she came to ecstasy. I tossed my head back as my own orgasm tore through my body and spilled into her center. My thumb circled her clit once and we both fell into oblivion.

 I pulled her satiated body to mine. She fit perfectly against me. I placed a delicate kiss where her neck and shoulder met. I let my head fall back to the pillow and enjoyed the feel of her in my arms. This was exactly what I had been missing. A living connection that grew thicker every moment we spent together.

 "Night, Mack. Thank you for catering to those hungry women tonight."

 "It was my pleasure. My pockets are fat with tips."

 She let out a phony laugh. "I bet they are——heaving with phone numbers, too. They were a horny bunch, grabbing at you like a bunch of hussies."

 I chuckled. "Were you jealous?"

 "Not in the least."

 The snippy tone in her voice betrayed her statement.

"All they did was make me want you more. I had counted down the minutes until we closed so that I could have my way with you. You are my girl, the only one I want beneath me, straddling me and moaning my name."

She said nothing but I could feel her relax further against me. I smiled against the pillow. I loved that she was jealous. I could mark this down in the book as the first time she was ever jealous. The fact that she had worked herself up over watching me with those women proved that she cared for me. My heart and feelings bloomed from her innocent reaction. She drove me nuts with her independence and commitment fears. I didn't want to contain her or keep her as a possession. I wanted only her love. My parents had never given two shits about me. For the first time in my life, I wanted someone to love me without conditions. Once I secured that, everything else would fall into place. I wasn't an idiot and I knew that relationships weren't all roses. Every relationship had its ups and downs. We would be no different. The desire to have it all with her burned in my chest. I wanted to tell her that I loved her but I wouldn't. She would have to be the one to say it first. My confidence soared because I knew that she would––eventually.

With regret, I left my beauty sleeping. I placed a kiss on her lips. She groggily responded with some words that weren't even in the English language. I chuckled on my way to work. The new door locks were in place. She would be safe. If I had stayed around the apartment, she would have thought that I was impeding on her ability to take care of herself. I would be the leech slowly sucking the independence from her soul. She was a feisty one who held on to false ideals with a death grip.

I walked through the office doors like a boss––well

because I am and I owned that shit. I rounded the corner, heading to my office, when a petite tornado of blonde hair twirled my way.

"Unci Mack, Unci Mack," Riley shouted as she swirled and danced her way to me.

I hauled the twisting toddler into my arms and hugged her tightly. The scent of baby powder and sugar drifted all around me. It was such a sweet and innocent smell that brought the world back into focus.

"Hey, Monkey. I've missed you." I inhaled her pureness one last time before I set her down.

"You wanna know what?" The depths of her blue eyes burned brightly.

"What?"

"I weally love you." She giggled.

"You wanna know what?" I repeated.

"What?" She continued to giggle

"I love you more."

I planted a smacking kiss on her cheek right before she dashed off, heading back toward her daddy's office. Her twinkling laughter rang in my ears long after she had rounded the corner and disappeared. With a little more pep in my step, I followed.

I walked through Forrest's office and patted Candice on the rump in a purely game coach manner. "Good game."

"Mack," she squealed.

I knew it would fire Forrest up. He was too easy to goad.

"Keep your dirty mitts to yourself," he growled.

My face split into the widest grin. I plopped next to Riley on the couch and leaned over to see what my lovely goddaughter was watching. I had assumed it would be some princess movie. I pulled her to my lap, amazed at her movie choice.

"Kylo Ren is my favorite character."

Her doe eyes widened further. "Mine too."

This kid had sunk her last claw in. I thought she had already fully entrenched herself into my heart but she managed to dig even deeper.

I could hear the muffled ringing of my phone deep in my pocket. I was enjoying my time with Riley so I let it ring. The ringing ceased. If they wanted a call back, they would leave a voicemail. Not even a second later, my phone rang again. I set Riley next to me so I could grab the damn thing.

"Yeah," I said testily.

"I've got another present. You need to come back home."

Abbie's spooked voice set me on high alert. I had been so immersed with Riley that Abbie's safety was put in to the back recesses of my mind. I can't believe I had been that stupid.

"Keep the doors locked until I get there. Breathe, baby. I'm on my way."

I hung up the phone and glanced over at Forrest. He nodded his understanding. I would fill him in later.

ABBIE 16

WITH MACK ON HIS WAY, my anxiety level drastically dropped. My hands still shook as the package lay inches away. I could see the mangled contents from the corner of my eye. After the initial shock began to wear off, anger seeped in. I didn't deserve this. Hell, no one deserved to be targeted this way. It angered and confused me that someone thought that this was okay.

I glanced up, annoyed, when the door flew open to where my scarred knight stood menacingly. Anyone in his or her right frame of mind would be petrified of him. I, on the other hand, was completely turned on. *What the hell did that say about me?* My heart skipped a beat and then beat as fast as a frightened horse. Blood rushed to my loins, setting them on fire. My skin felt too tight against my bones as goose bumps rose upon my arms. I shivered with desire strong enough to self-combust.

His large frame stalked toward me. It felt as though I had looked at miles of strong and toned skin before I landed on his worried-filled eyes. It had been a long time since anyone had cared for me that much. I wanted to grab hold of him and unleash a torrential river of tears but I wouldn't. I needed him to erase the images that had been burned into my mind. Before he even had a chance to look inside the box, I swiped the box from the table, spilling the mangled doll pieces all over the kitchen floor. I stood and wrapped my body around him, forcing him to focus on me.

"We can go over this later. Right now, I need you," I whispered in his ear.

He kept silent as he walked us to the bedroom, where he gently laid me upon the bed. His gaze warmed a path from my toes to my cheeks. I sat up and freed myself of my clothing. His hawk-like eyes never left my body. He had watched every move I made. The grin that spread across his face was predatory and made my toes curl.

My body and soul were freely open for him to take. I had never loved a man in his entirety. Sure, I loved cock but never the person it was attached to. Mack knew how to work his and I loved every thick inch of it. But, it was more than that. I loved the way he spoke to me as though he were truly interested. I loved the way that his concern for me overshadowed his own safety. I even loved the way that his caveman instincts flowed over into my life. I never felt restricted by his presence. I was a free spirit and he let me roam. My heart thundered beneath my breasts at the realization that I loved this man and it scared me more than any damage a stalker could invoke.

He slid between my legs and kissed a path from my navel to each breast. As his teeth grazed my sensitive nipple, my back arched. I moaned from each tingling sensation his mouth brought. He was a sinful package and all mine to unwrap. His mouth covered mine. I opened for him, letting my tongue mate with his. His kisses were a slow drug that encased my body, making me feel heavy and intoxicated. Every time I was with him, the world disappeared. My brain shut down when his strong hands touched me. All I could focus on was him and how he made my body soar with every kiss.

I rolled his chiseled body beneath mine. I straddled his hips, kissing my way down his chest. His bulging cock demanded entrance as I hovered over his hips. I reached between our bodies and guided his cock toward my entrance. I slid down his shaft as he pushed through my opening. I tossed my head back, sighing as his cock filled me. He pushed his hips up as I rocked back and forth. The minor pain from his thick cock quickly dissolved into a drugging pleasure. His hands reached for my breasts, urging me to quicken my pace. His rough fingers drew more pleasure. With every tweak, my core sung his praise.

"Fuck, Abbie," he swore through clenched teeth.

"Yes, baby. All mine." I hadn't meant to say that aloud but it had been said and I could not take it back. In this moment, he was mine. He was tangible and something that I could hold fast to as my world spun out of control. Scared to love him, scared that he would get hurt, and terrified that he would be taken from me too soon, I showed him my love the only way I knew how, by throwing us both off the cliff and into the vivid depths of ecstasy.

We sat around the table and examined the pieces from the package I had opened earlier. There were no markings on the outside of the box and no note inside. I had no clue as to who had sent this to me. I looked to Mack to find some understanding. His blank face offered nothing.

"Does this mangled doll mean that he wants to cut me into tiny pieces?" My voice portrayed sarcasm but deep inside I wanted to hide.

"I don't know but he won't get close enough to you to even try." The look in his eyes hardened. "I'll kill that sick son-of-a-bitch before he harms one hair on your head."

My laughter took on a hysterical tone. "You can't protect me from everything. What if you get hurt in the process?" I rubbed my temples, trying to alleviate the beginning of a headache. "I can't live with knowing that I had inadvertently put your life in danger."

The right thing to do was to let him go. He didn't deserve this way of life. He deserved to have a life without worrying about constant danger.

His head zipped to the side forcefully. "Just what are you trying to say?"

I sighed heavily with the weight of my decision. "I'm saying that we are over."

"Are you serious?" he bellowed.

I straightened my spine. This was how it had to be. My stalker would not come out of hiding unless Mack was gone. I had to distance myself from him and from everyone else I loved.

"Yes."

He pushed the chair back so hard that it crashed to the floor as he stood. "This isn't over."

His authoritative tone only further sealed my decision. I watched him with deep sadness as he stomped out of the door. I slumped back in my chair and let all of my bottled-up emotions run down my cheeks. The sharp pains that had settled in my chest shortly after Mack had walked out the door had not dissipated. I had sat at the kitchen table until the pink hues promised a better tomorrow. I stood and stretched my body until all of the aches and pains were tolerable. I boxed the rest of my feelings inside and got ready for work. That mother-fucker may have won that round but by God, I was going to win his game and take my life back.

I called Marie before I headed downstairs.

"Hey, girl," she answered on the first ring.

I could hear Lia screaming in the background. It was hard to tell whether she was happy or pissed off at Marie.

"What did you do to piss off your niece now?" I laughed.

"I told her she had to keep her clothes on."

I imagined that she was rolling her eyes, which made me laugh that much harder.

"Oh, it gets better."

I stopped laughing long enough to ask, "Really? Do tell."

"We were having a conversation about how many ear-rings I had, when she said to me, I don't have earrings but I have nipples. Then she pulled off her shirt and showed me. Oh my God, I was dying. I told her that it was inappropriate to show her nipples and to put her shirt back on. That's when you called."

The laughter came in droves. I couldn't stop it was too hilarious.

"Let me know when you are done," she sarcastically spat between her own laughter.

I held on to my stomach. "Okay, okay. I think I'm done now. Seriously though, she is a pistol."

"I'm afraid that when I have kids they are going to be ten times worse than her. I don't think I should procre-ate."

"You have to. I need a good laugh now and again."

"Yeah, I'll get right on that just for you. Anyhoo, what's up?"

"I know that this is spur of the moment but are you

working this weekend?"

"Actually, I'm not. What do you have in mind?"

"I was thinking a girl's trip."

"By plane or by car?"

"By car. Nothing too far but far enough to get out of town for a night."

"Sounds good. Do you have a destination in mind?"

"Nope. Not yet. Let me know if you have any ideas."

"All right. I'm gonna let you go. I can't even hear myself think right now."

"Later, girl."

I hung up, still giggling from Lia's outburst. Spending time with my girl would surely lift my spirits. It had been ages since the two of us hung out. We were getting too old to go out clubbing like a bunch of twenty-year-olds. A nice winery sounded like the best way to spend the weekend. There was a place a couple of hours out of town that had received good reviews. I sent her a quick text.

LET'S GO TO THE OLIVER INN AND WINERY.

I didn't expect a response until after Lia left. She had her hands full.

I was hoping that tonight the bar wouldn't be packed. I had to make sure every employee was on staff this weekend. I seldom left the bar but I'm sure that everyone would be on board. The tips alone would be enticing enough. The darkened bar lit up like the streets of Vegas after I flipped the switch. I loved the dark-to-light trans-formation. It felt less lonely and barren once I turned the lights on. I also loved the bar's seductive lure when I dimmed the lights. This place was my home but I was in dire need of a break.

Curtis trudged through the doors. He was usually a weekender. Coming in during the week wasn't typical behavior for him.

"Hi, Curtis. What can I get you?"

"Hey, Abbie. Whatever you have on tap is fine."

My concern for him grew. He never ordered from the tap. It was always a bottle. The brand never mattered as long as it wasn't on draft. I threw him a bone and opened up a Coors and set it in front of him.

"Care to unload?" I asked, curious to see whether he would.

He looked up at me with bloodshot eyes. "My wife asked for a divorce."

Hell, he had stumped me. For a second there, I thought he said *wife*. I have never heard him speak of her name. Tells you how well I knew my customers. I mentally shook off my surprise.

"Well shit, Curtis, that sucks."

A smile adorned his face. "That it does. I know I can be a prick." He blew out a frustrated sigh. "This came out of left field. She gave no indication that she was unhappy. Fuck, Abbie, I don't want her to leave."

I looked him dead in the eye. "Then what the fuck are you doing here drinking? Get your ass back home and listen to your wife. Find out what she needs from you to stick the marriage out."

He grabbed his wallet and I waved him away. "It's on the house. Now get."

I swatted him with the dishtowel.

He chugged the remnants of his beer and hightailed it out as though his ass were on fire. He had a lot of groveling to do. I had a strong feeling that his wife would make him jump through a bunch of hoops before she made her decision.

Patrons slowly trickled in and out for the rest of the evening. I was glad that the bar was steady and not too busy. I was able to contact all my employees and set the weekend up to be fully staffed. The only face I wanted to see never walked in. I know that I had said it was over but that didn't make me miss him any less. Marie shot me a text later that evening, saying that she was on board. At least I had that to look forward to.

I lay in bed and tossed and turned. After a heated debate in my head I grabbed the pillow that Mack slept with. I switched mine out with his. His scent barely lingered but it helped lull me to sleep. I jerked awake from the sound of a text coming through my phone. I quickly snatched it, hoping that it was from Mack. The number was blocked. I opened it up anyway.

GET SOME REST, MY ANGEL. YOU'RE GOING TO NEED IT. SWEET DREAMS.

I threw the phone across the room. *How the hell did he get my number?* I tossed the covers off and ran to check all of the door locks. I blew out a breath of unease. Everything was locked up tight and yet the feeling of being watched intensified. I grabbed the only sharp knife I owned and sat erect, clutching my weapon.

MACK 17

I WAS FUCKING FURIOUS WITH ABBIE. *How dare she push me away!* Afraid for my safety? What a crock of shit. If she knew half of what I'd done, she would want me attached to her hip. Her fear of her stalker was real. Her feelings for me frightened her more. I would keep my distance but I sure as hell wouldn't keep her unprotected.

"Forrest, when are those guys showing up?" I hollered through the office.

"Within the hour," he said from the doorway of my office.

That motherfucker was deadly silent. "I'd like to put Holt and Knox on her detail tonight."

"What she do––kick you to the curb?"

An astute asshole! I grinned. "She sure did."

"She didn't take long to get sick of your ugly mug. I think it's the scar. It screams look at how tough I am."

"Fuck you. That scar seduces all the ladies."

He laughed. "More like pity for how big of a baby you are. See you in the conference room in an hour."

I'd really like to throat punch him. Watching him clutch at his throat and gasping for air would brighten my day exponentially. It was in the bro code: physical beatings on a regular basis were highly encouraged for emotional release.

While I waited for the rest of the guys, I tried to call Abbie but it went straight to voicemail. She was probably still sleeping so I shot a text to her.

LET ME KNOW YOU ARE ALL RIGHT.

Her quick response told me that she was screening my calls.

FINE.

Fuck it. I tossed my phone on the desk and went over the files on our new recruits.

The troop pounded into the office like a herd of elephants. Their laughter rang out through the halls. Their energy was infectious. I couldn't help but become energized from the new team members. Fresh faces and fresh meat––I could smell the new blood.

We all congregated in the conference room and shook hands.

"Now that we've all showed our dicks, let's get down to business."

Forrest wasn't a broad guy but when he took charge, he puffed himself out like a cobra.

"Landon and Shep, we have the senator in town and they requested extra men. You two will stick to him like glue. His normal security isn't too happy about it but you have top clearance. He has a couple of committee meetings and a dinner. You start tomorrow. Any questions?"

"Nope. I'm down for an easy assignment," Landon piped in.

Forrest looked sharply at Shep. "No Hawaiian shirt––blend in."

"Well you just took the fun out of the job, boss man. I'll keep it clean since this is the first assignment. I can't promise that I won't stir up shit on the next one."

Shep was going to turn into a liability. We all might go down in flames with him on board but it would be one hell of a ride.

"Holt and Knox, you will be providing protection for Abbie James. I've set her file in front of you. Your presence is to be minimal and unseen. Holt, you will take morning shift and Knox, you will be on night duty. She is being stalked and we have no evidence as to who it is. Be on high alert to anything suspicious. Mack will be in and around and can take over if anyone needs a break. Your detail will start tonight."

"Is she hot?" Holt asked.

"Don't even think about it. She's mine," I gritted through my teeth.

"Seems to me that you wouldn't need us if she wanted you," Holt shot off.

As quick as lightning, I was out of my chair and throwing Holt to the ground. I punched him in the nose and then wrapped my hands around his throat. He swung, jabbing me in the kidney. I loosened my hold to take another swipe at his GQ face when I was physically forced off him.

"You good, Holt?" Forrest asked.

"Yep. I was just getting warmed up." He cracked his knuckles.

"Damn, my money was on Scarface," Shep said, disappointed that the fight ended too quickly.

"As you can see, Mack is a little unhinged when it comes to Abbie. Let's keep it professional, boys."

Forrest let go of me. I stood in the exact spot, trying to gain control. When the red disappeared, I walked over to Holt. I squeezed him on the shoulder. "You've got a hell of a kidney punch. You almost put me out of commission. We good?"

"Yep, just testing the waters. You've got a solid right hook." He chuckled.

"You all have your assignments. You are free to go," Forrest boomed.

His cold amber eyes kept me rooted in place. I guess I was the only one not free to go. Once the guys had cleared out, I took a seat and waited for him to lay into me for acting like a prepubescent boy. *Shit!* He was going to unleash something unholy by the way the silence settled heavily in the room.

"I want you clear-headed. Go take a run or a hefty shit. I don't give a fuck. You are my partner, not my damn son. I shouldn't have to have this conversation with you. Quit thinking with your dick."

I hung my head in shame.

"I don't know how to separate the two, when it comes to her," I mumbled.

"Figure it out or you'll both be in the morgue."

He left me in solitude with his sweet parting words hanging morbidly in the air. I'd have rather him kick my ass. I deserved nothing less. *When did I become a whiney bitch?* It's as though I were walking through a tunnel filled with my Ruby's siren. I couldn't determine what was what. I was drowning in her. I couldn't afford to continue down this path. Forrest was right; if I did, we would both be dead. It was time to man up and reacquaint myself with my field training. I was too emotionally involved. I had to separate myself from her and treat her as a client. I would do so until the job was done and she was secure. Hopefully when it was all said and done, I could win her back.

ABBIE 18

I STARTED AWAKE. I LOOKED DOWN and sure enough, the kitchen knife had dropped to the floor. I bent over and picked up my flimsy choice of weapon and set it on the coffee table. It would do in a pinch. I would have to get something with a little more stopping power and longer range. I bounced up with my light bulb moment and ran straight to my father's closet. On the tips of my toes, I reached toward the top shelf and felt around until my fingers touched the metal box. I pulled it down and sat on the bed.

I rubbed the top of the box lovingly, swirling the dust around in circles. My father believed that human nature was mostly kind. However, he told me once, that it didn't hurt to have a gun stowed away just in case. I unlatched the clip and peered at the very thing that would save me. As I stared at the gun, a sense of tranquility came over me. A hint of oak moss and lavender surrounded me.

"Hey, Dad. I miss you." I sniffed. "I hope you are dancing and laughing with Mom."

Maybe I was going mad or maybe my dad was here to comfort me. I chose to believe the latter. Ever since his passing, I could feel his presence. He usually came around when I was stressed and longed for the safety of his arms.

I set the box on the bed and scooted up to his pillows. "You always gave the best hugs. I wish you were here to give me some guidance with Mack. I'm in love with him but I'm afraid it will end tragically, like you and Mom." Tears slid down my cheeks. "I might not live through whoever is stalking me. It wouldn't be fair to Mack. Daddy, I didn't want to push him away but I had no choice. I know he can protect me better than I ever could but if he got hurt or worse, I would never recover."

A musky scent flowed heavily around me. I could almost imagine him sitting next to me, running his fingers through my hair just like he did when I was a little girl. I lay there, basking in his love until the smell disappeared.

"I love you. Daddy. Thank you," I whispered.

I returned the knife to the drawer and texted Marie.

I'LL PICK YOU UP TOMORROW MORNING. BE READY.

I'LL BE READY.

Feeling less pitiful, I got ready for my last night of work.

We were headed down the highway with the windows down and the music blaring. A gigantic lip-splitting grin transformed my face as I peeked over at Marie. I laughed heartily as she practically screeched out the lyrics. Freedom laced my blood, making me giddy. With every rotation of the tires, we headed closer to relaxation.

"I'm glad you dragged me away. I needed this." Marie sighed as she turned down the radio.

"Dragged you away? It didn't take much to convince

you to come along." I chuckled.

"Po-tay-toe, pu-tah-to. It was a brilliant idea. I'm thankful for your spontaneity. After a couple glasses of wine, you'll reveal the real reason."

"Whatever. We both needed to get away and you know it."

"I'm not disagreeing." She put her feet up on the dashboard. "It's been a couple of years since the two of us said the hell with it and left for some R&R."

"We both have busy schedules and it worked out this time. We should schedule a weekend getaway more frequently."

"Now you're talking."

MACK 19

I SCREWED MY HEAD ON STRAIGHT and headed to meet with Holt to see what was cooking. I didn't even get a chance to get out of my car when Abbie walked out of her building. Not wanting to miss the opportunity to see where my little Ruby was headed, I followed. I called Holt and told him to bug off, that I had her once I realized that she was headed south of town. I put in a call to Forrest and let him know that they had stopped at a winery. I would continue the detail until they got back. He probably had a list of shit to keep Holt and Knox busy until we returned. Whenever that would be. It looked like a girls' getaway but for how long I didn't know. *Looks as if I would be wine tasting or whatever women did at places like this.* I hated wine.

I slid up to the desk after they had checked in and were headed up to their room. I sweet-talked the receptionist into giving me a room right next door to them. I wish I were that charming; it was more like I passed myself off as an ignorant wine connoisseur trying to understand why my wife enjoys this shit. I threw in a possible anniversary date and extend my knowledge before booking––yada, yada, yada.

I took my time canvasing the lobby and exits. I wanted to give them enough time to get to their room before I headed up. No sense in giving myself away by running into them. I turned toward the gift shop, hoping they would have some clothing in my size. Needless to say, there was no preparation for this trip. I walked out of the shop with my new character's clothing. I hoped I wouldn't stand out but let's just say that there wasn't a wide selection. I was a pretty big dude and couldn't just pick up any old shirt without the back ripping out on me.

I stood in front of the bed and examined my purchases. I hoped I could write this shit off. My bank account was mocking me. Gone were my favorite jeans, replaced with a pair of khakis that were a bit too snug. I had to adjust my junk just looking at them lying on the bed. A multi-colored plaid dress shirt, some fake reader glasses, and a hat to help hide my scar finished off my outfit. Thankfully I kept my sneakers on this morning.

My ears perked up when I heard giggling. The rooms were simple and comfortable. What I loved about this room was that the walls were paper-thin. I could only hear their muffled words but it was enough to know when they were in their room and when they were leaving. Unfortunately, I didn't have my equipment with me so I had to rely on the walls to whisper their secrets.

Dressed in my new attire, I followed them. I stayed far enough back and enjoyed the view of Abbie's delicious backside. My body itched to get closer and touch what was mine. She stumbled but quickly caught herself. She twisted to look over her shoulder. I ducked my head, stuck my hands in my pocket and slowed my pace. I chanced a look from beneath the rim of my hat and they were laughing hysterically at her faux pas. I grinned in solidarity. Watching her become carefree was enchanting. I became hooked all over again. Her laughter was deep and throaty and beckoned me. What a web she had spun. I was the fly caught helpless, no longer struggling to get free. I accepted my fate, waiting for her lethal dose.

The room was small and intimate. Everyone seemed excited and talked rapidly about the tasting. I was a novice. I sat there and observed the scene. The waiters and waitresses began with the first round. I watched the other people at my table breathe in and hold the wine in their mouth before they swallowed. I slammed it back like a shot. Huge mistake. I wanted to gag but held it back as the burn of the wine stuck in my throat. This shit was like drinking the cheapest bourbon. It was a mixture of hairspray and too much old lady perfume.

I peeked over at Abbie's table and she had a contemplative look on her pinup features. I assumed that she had come to the same findings as I had. The wine flowed steadily throughout the afternoon and well into the evening. About the fifth wine, some of my table companions started to spit it out. I was in some kind of crazy dimension. I had been taught that spitting was a deplorable act. Here a bunch of wine snobs were spitting quite frequently and no one was even fazed. Hell, if they were spitting out this disgusting shit, so the fuck was I.

For the final wine, they asked us to put on our blindfolds. Hell to the no was I participating in that. I politely refused––with minimal growling––as everyone else slid the fabric over their eyes. It was the perfect opportunity to get close and have a little fun with Abbie. I walked up to the waiter and asked to serve their table. Actually, I slipped him a couple of hundreds. He happily complied. I only wanted a minute to be near her.

I stood close to Abbie's side, barely touching her shoulder with my hip.

I bent closer to her ear and seductively whispered, "A vintage, sweet, red wine that will send your taste buds into a frenzy and your body quivering for more." I reached for her trembling hand and smoothed her fingers around the stem of the glass. Her breath hitched when our fingers came together. The craving to haul her back to my room hit me square in the solar plexus. I straightened and walked out of the room. I kept an eye on her as I tamped my own desires.

She removed her blindfold, twisting her body from side to side, and searched for me. My eyes locked onto hers from the hall. The moment felt surreal. I wanted her to see me and to know that I would always be there. I enjoyed the surprise as well as the lust that swirled in her darkened eyes. I could almost feel the race of her pulse and the desire that she kept contained. I broke the gaze and disappeared to a spot where I could continue to watch but she could no longer see me.

ABBIE 20

I TOOK DEEP BREATHS IN AND out, trying to slow my beating heart. I didn't want Marie to know that Mack was here and how much his presence had stirred me up. I should've known that he would stay in the background even when I told him to leave. As turned on as I was, I also felt relieved and safe. Throughout our time here I had laughed at the appropriate times and said all of the right things. I didn't want to ruin this trip for Marie. I had asked her to come and I wouldn't burden her with my worries. I had been enjoying myself but the fears never kept silent. The minute I heard him speak every one of those worries immediately dissolved into nothingness. I longed to go to Mack. I wanted his arms to hold me tight while his lips kissed every inch of my flesh. It took all of my strength to stay rooted to my chair and continue on as though he hadn't awakened every lustful cell in my body.

"Which bottle or four are we taking back to our room?"

I smiled at my best friend, attempting to push Mack's presence to the farthest recesses of my mind. "I'm going to get a damn case of the last one we tasted. I almost had an orgasm in my mouth."

We ordered a couple of bottles for our room. Marie was shocked when I ordered a case to be sent to my house.

"I didn't think you were serious. You're such a lush." She laughed.

"I'm not gonna share an ounce of it either!"

"Stingy bitch."

"You know it."

We drank until the wee hours of the morning. Not once did I bring up Mack or the stalker. We reminisced of days gone by. My body still lusted for Mack but I managed to ignore my raging hormones and had an awesome time remembering all of the stupid things that we had done. The million and one sleepovers that we still had to this day.

"Do you remember almost hitting that cow out in bum-fuck-Egypt?"

"Oh my God, that was a close call. What about the time where we slept in the back of your Jeep, freezing, because we had been drinking and couldn't go home? I couldn't smell Bailey's for a long time after that."

"How many times did we watch the *Buffy* reruns? That guy is still hot!"

We were both in stitches with every story we told.

With each memory, the long-standing fibers of our friendship grew stronger. I couldn't find a memory that she hadn't been a part of and vice versa. We had been fast friends for twenty-six years. There were periods where we had gone days and months without talking but we always managed to come together again as though no time at all had passed. We had both laughed and cried happy tears well into the night.

Marie took the driver seat while I submerged myself in the passenger role. The lush scenery passed without so much as a glance. I focused on the vehicle that had pulled out behind us from the inn. The driver had stayed far enough back to not raise any suspicions. Since Mack had revealed himself the other night, I knew it was his shadowed frame behind the steering wheel.

Marie pulled up along the curb outside of her house. I hopped out of the car to give her a hug.

"Thanks for coming with me. Next time our trip will be longer." I squeezed her tightly.

"It was much needed. I'm glad you came up with the idea. Love you, girl."

"Love you too."

The truck no longer followed behind. I lost sight of it once we hit town. I drove back to my place, eager to be by myself. I thought about going into work tonight but I nixed the idea just as quickly as it had popped in my head. They would survive without me for another night. I made a tight U-turn and headed to Dispenza's to grab a pizza. I didn't feel like cooking. Pizza and a bottle of my new wine sounded like heaven.

I dropped the pizza box as I read the kindergarten scratch taped to my door.

I'M SORRY I MISSED YOU. UNTIL NEXT TIME.

I screamed at the door and tore the note into tiny pieces. I threw the tiny shreds of paper and watched them float to the wood boards. I jumped and turned in the direction of a deep male voice.

"Excuse me, miss?" The male voice boomed through the tight stairwell.

I could barely see the features of the figure who stood at the bottom of the stairs. He was tall and wiry. That's all that I could make out from the shadows of the stairwell.

"Stop. Do not come any closer," I commanded.

My nerves were completely shot. *He could be my stalker.*

"I'm sorry to disturb you. I was walking by and heard

a scream. Are you alright?"

He seemed genuine but I couldn't afford to make any kind of assumption.

"I'm fine. Thank you for checking."

"Yes, ma'am."

I turned back around, grabbed my mangled pizza box and dashed through the front door. I leaned heavily on the door, taking deep breaths. I put the box on the table and grabbed the knife. Every room was empty and had no sign of being disturbed. I opened the nightstand drawer. The gun was nestled in the same place. I double-checked all the doors to make sure they were locked, and grabbed the pizza and the remaining two bottles of wine.

A week had gone by with not a single word from Mack. I hadn't called either but had almost caved in to the urge multiple times. It was my fault but my anger grew exponentially with each passing minute that he hadn't reached out to me. I could feel him out there but he was still too far away for my liking. I couldn't sleep. I was turning into a walking zombie. It was so bad, everyone I encountered at the bar asked whether someone had died. *Yeah, my fucking heart did*. I was ornery as fuck; even Marie had called me a bitch and told me to go get laid.

The only person who didn't find me repulsive was a guy who had started coming in a couple of days ago. He screamed farm strong. He was definitely not a gym rat. He always sat facing the door and ordered one Rolling Rock every hour. He would stay until last call and promptly get up and leave. Curiosity had finally drove me to stand in front of him after handing him his beer.

"Got a name?" I asked, in a surprisingly non-bitchy tone.

He stared at the bottle as he answered. "Knox. You are?"

"Abbie. Bet your girl can't get a word in with all that talking you do, Knox. It's nice to meet you."

His strong chin rose from his chest. His eyes latched on to me with a hint of mischievousness. "Can't say that I have one. You interested?"

His innocent flirtations cracked me up. "I'm not your type."

"No, you're not. You're beautiful but you have that look of 'already taken' written all over you."

I laughed at the absurdity. "Nope. Single."

"Interesting. So, do you want to hook up?"

I genuinely laughed at him. The tone of his voice was insincere. "Are you new around here? I can't say that I've ever seen you before."

"You could say that."

"In town for business, pleasure, or trouble?"

"All of the above." He chuckled.

"Well, it's a small town. I'm sure you'll find all three of those."

I looked up, giddy as Marie blew through the doors. *Speak of trouble and in it walks.*

"Hey, girl. Pour me a stiff one. I had this client—"

The words died on her lips as she got a good look at the hunk of meat sitting in front of me.

"Who is your new friend, Abs?" Her voice went silky.

I rolled my eyes as I looked back at Knox.

"This is Knox. Knox, that's the irritating best friend of mine, also known as Marie."

She stuck out her hand demurely, practically purring. "Pleasure."

What the hell was that? I had seen her hook-up game a million times and this was not in her box of tricks!

"Pleasure is all mine." His lips met the top of her hand and kissed the skin smoothly.

Holy shit. I had now entered the twilight zone. Marie had completely gone off her rocker and I had entered the *Gone With The Wind* era. I went and made her martini, no longer interested in their banter.

I rudely interrupted them. "So, this client of yours?"

She ignored me for a full minute before her squeals of spreading gossip erupted.

"Let me retract that statement. It wasn't my client per-se; it was her mother. The girl was getting her hair done for prom and wanted all of these loose curls; with it half up and half down, right?" She took a huge gulp of air. "Well, I get her hair all curled and styled and this girl just beamed at the do. She adored it. That is, until her mother came back to my booth for a look and tore the style to shreds. It was styled sophisticatedly and yet with the youthful look. I have to say she looked awesome."

I laughed when she literally patted herself on the back.

"Her mother went on a tirade. She yelled at the top of her lungs that her daughter looked like a call girl. She told me to redo it and if it wasn't done correctly, she wouldn't pay me. Seriously, I wanted to bitch slap her. What an ugly bitch. I felt so damn bad for the young lady sitting in the chair. If I could adopt her, I would've. So I spent another hour braiding and tucking it up so that she looked like some innocent five-year-old. It still looked pretty but not as good as the first time." She huffed out a breath.

"Damn! What a way to ruin the girl's night. I bet she still loved her style, though."

"She did and she apologized for her mother too. I bet

she is wishing to escape that hell hole."

"I'd already have my bags packed."

We both giggled. Then she ignored me again to strike up a conversation with Knox. After a while, they were the only two left in the bar. I eventually kicked them out the door and closed shop, feeling even lonelier than before.

As I lay in bed, another text pinged.

ARE YOU READY FOR ME? I'M COMING FOR YOU, SOON.

I typed back, furious.

BRING IT ON, FUCKER.

I can't explain what prompted me to say something that bold to such a demented person. I know I was only egging him on. I was ready for this shit to be over with. I didn't have a death wish. I simply was sick and tired of feeling helpless. I wanted a confrontation, no matter the ending. The need to come face to face with my harasser spurred me on.

SOON, MY ANGEL. SOON.

I put my phone on silent and shoved it across the bed. *Let him try to get me.* I was ready. I had gone back to my jujitsu instructor and further honed my skills. During the day, I exhausted my body, committing all of the moves to muscle memory. My instructor drilled me until my arms and legs were liquefied Jell-o. When he came to get me, I would give him the fight of his life. I wouldn't go down crying and begging for my life. Nope. I would go down in a hail of badassary. My father's gun had become a constant companion. I ceased dressing in my pinup style for work. I dressed comfortably so that I could move freely and hide my gun. At night, I slept in workout pants and a tank, with the gun tucked safely under my pillow. *Yeah,*

I yawned, *I'll open up the door, grinning for that motherfucker. Let him see who the real predator was.*

MACK 21

MY LITTLE RUBY WAS PREPARING for war. I was so damn proud of her that I was about to explode. I watched her get more badass every day. Her jujitsu was impressive. I was eager to roll around on the mat with her. Her range skills improved every time she went to practice. Holt and Knox had become enamored with her as well. When I wasn't watching her, they kept me well informed. Knox had taken to her more than any other individual he had ever protected. I'd trust Knox to do what was necessary to keep her safe. My concern for her was still on high alert and we never truly left her alone. I knew in my heart that if I couldn't get right to her, she would hold her own until I could rip the fucker's balls off.

She had never contacted me about any other threats but that didn't mean they weren't there. Holt had heard her scream the day that they had come back from the winery but she had said that she was fine. He had brought back the ripped paper for us to examine. It was clear that her stalker was increasing the stakes. We hadn't kept watch on her place while she was gone. We could not have afforded to make that mistake. If we had been, we could have caught the bastard or at least got a good look at who he was and kept an eye on him. That was the last threat that we knew of. The day after that, she had started prepping. Which led me to believe that the threats were still coming and frequently. The waiting was driving me nuts.

I took on a restoration project for Enzo to keep my mind clear. During the mornings, I went over to his shop and put my hands to work. His family had wormed their way in to my life. They were always popping in and out of the shop. My favorite was his mom, Roselva. God, she was brash and I adored her. She was the mother I had never had but longed for.

"Son, when are you going to whisk that girl off her feet? She looks like she lost her best friend."

My insides warmed when she called me son. "Soon. Just waiting for the right time. How do you know these things? I never told you about her."

"Madone! You men are dense. You wait too long and someone else is going to snatch her away from you. I have my ways on finding information that I deem important."

"You mean gossiping," Enzo commented.

"Watch your mouth. You're not too big to throw over my knee."

"Yes, ma'am."

I laughed at their exchange. Her hand came out of nowhere and smacked me upside the head, albeit lovingly. She waddled back toward Enzo, pecked him on the cheek and left. To grow up in that household would have been a blast. I had to thank my negligent parents. Without their lack of guidance, I wouldn't be where I am today. That's the only thing I will ever thank them for.

"What are you waiting for?" Enzo asked from across the room.

"For her to realize that she can't live without me." I chuckled but I was as serious as the sun rises.

"Momma was right––you are dense. I didn't give my woman an ounce of breathing room and we are going on fifteen blissful years."

"Not all of us can be so lucky. I got a plan. Don't you worry––"

The door opened with gusto. "I almost forgot, dinner at my house next weekend. Don't be late. Mack, you better be there with Abbie or don't come at all," she cackled. And slammed the door shut.

"Your mom is hilarious!"

"She is serious. If you don't bring Abbie to dinner, she will pitch a fit and you probably won't be invited back."

"Damn. I'll have to figure this out. I may have to pass."

"I wouldn't do that either. You don't want to be on Momma's bad side. Trust me on that one." He laughed uncontrollably.

"I don't know why you are laughing––you're the one related to her."

"Very true but she has ways of making your life miserable if she wanted to, related or not."

"I'm sure she can. That's why I'm going to get back to work and worry about dinner another time."

"Smart man!"

I finished the dresser and started on the bedframe. Enzo had a plethora of projects that he had going on. Some were customer orders and others were odds and ends that he had picked up at garage and estate sales. Those pieces went into his shop for sale. Those were the pieces that I worked on. I could pick and choose which ones I wanted to do and take my time. We didn't have an employee contract. He allowed me to come in whenever I wanted and to work as long as I wanted. If he sold the pieces, I would get a percentage of the sale. That was good enough for me. I told him I didn't want any money but he insisted. So, that was the agreement that we shook on.

I locked up the shop and went to go check on Knox. He would be on duty and ready to head into the bar. I wanted to catch him before he did. I liked the fact that he went inside to keep an eye on her. I parked behind Knox's car. I left the car running and stepped out. Knox had already opened his window. I leaned down.

"How's my girl?"

"She's doing well. Kicked her instructor's ass tonight. I think that she needs to find a better one. She is far more advanced." He snickered.

I chuckled. "Don't you even think about offering to teach her. She'd probably kick your ass too. I take it nothing has happened lately. I talked to Holt this morning and he hasn't seen or heard anything."

He shook his head. "Nada. I've been listening to the patrons and nothing. Everyone gets along with her. She knows most of the clientele. I don't know what this fucker is waiting for. It's starting to piss me off. I haven't seen anyone hanging around suspiciously, either. No one has lingered by her apartment or outside of the bar. Holt's said the same thing."

"This guy may have made us and is keeping a low profile, biding his time. Keep extra vigilant and if you or Holt need a break, let me know and I'll fill in. He is waiting for us to leave her unguarded. That's when he will strike. It's exactly what I would do. No gaps."

"You got it, boss."

"Call me if you need anything. I'm not far from here."

He nodded and I walked back to my car. I watched Knox get out and head inside. I picked up my phone and sent my girl a text. It had been a couple of days since I sent one. I couldn't have her thinking that I was over her.

YOU LOOK BEAUTIFUL TONIGHT. HOW ARE YOU?

I sat and waited for her reply. She may not take my calls but she would text me back.

READY TO TAKE ON THE WORLD.

I looked down and smiled.

HOW ABOUT YOU TAKE ME ON FIRST.

LOL. IN YOUR DREAMS.

IN EVERY DREAM. CARE TO MAKE IT A REALITY?

MACK...

ROSELVA INVITED US TO DINNER NEXT WEEK-END. THINK ABOUT IT.

I drove back to the shop. My plan to work her up backfired in my face. I wanted her back and she wasn't budging on her decision.

I sat on the stool, twirling around and around like a toddler in a doctor's office. As I was twirling around, a wooden box caught my eye. I put my boot on the floor and stopped the stool. I waited for the room to stop spinning before I checked out the box. If it was what I thought it was, then I just had a brilliant idea.

I delicately picked up the box and examined all the sides. The shape reminded me of an old cigar box but larger and deeper. This would be perfect for Abbie to hide her gun in plain sight. The box was void of any engraving. It was made out of cedar. I brought it to my nose and inhaled its rich scent. I opened it up, curious of its inner contents. *Wonderful——there was nothing I had to tear out.* I wonder why this had caught Enzo's eye. Regardless, I knew exactly what I was going to do with it.

I worked well into the night. The whole upper part of my body ached from working for hours hunched over. The box now looked as if it had been carved right out of a red cedar tree. The wood had been restored to its former glory. The aroma of the cedar grew intense with each swipe of the sanding block. If I finished this right, this feminine gun safe would be around much longer than I would. My engraving skills were mediocre at best but I was going to do it anyway. It may end up looking as though Riley had made it but I know she would cherish it anyway.

I stood and stretched. My neck and back popped and cracked as my body readjusted from sitting too long. I checked my phone. As I expected, Abbie had not responded to my text. I looked at the time. It was too late to stop in at Forrest's, so back to my empty apartment it was. I tried to spend as little time there as I could. Long enough to rest my head and clean up.

I was driving through the empty streets, heading home when I made a sudden left turn. I found myself parked next to Knox. I shouldn't be here and yet I made no move to drive away. I shut the car off and walked to the driver's side of Knox's car.

His window was already rolled down. "I'm going up. If you want to take off for the night, go ahead."

"Sure thing, boss."

I climbed the stairs and knocked on the door. The bar hadn't closed that long ago so I know that she hadn't fallen asleep yet. I could hear her light footsteps nearing the door. I imagined the long sigh that escaped her mouth and the gears in her mind cranking over as she debated on whether or not to open the door. It didn't matter whether she opened up or not. Her footsteps assured me that she was safe. I could go back to my car for the remainder of the night and keep her guarded, but for my peace of mind, I had to see her to make certain that she was truly doing as fine as her text said that she was. I was about to turn around when the door cracked open.

"Why are you here, Mack?" Her voice was laced with sadness.

I wanted to haul her into my arms but I maintained my distance. I didn't agree with her decision but I respected it.

"I needed to see for myself that you were okay. I can't decipher that through a text. Will you please let me in so I can talk to you?" I pleaded with her.

"I don't think that's a good idea. You know we will just end up in bed."

"Not that I wouldn't turn you down but I only want to have a conversation with you." I held up my hand. "Scout's honor."

A small, breathy chuckle escaped her lips. "Were you even in the Boy Scouts?"

"Let me in and I'll tell you." I moved closer to the door.

She hesitated briefly before she opened the door. I squeaked by in case she shut the door in my face. I breathed a sigh of relief as I walked through.

"Do you want anything to drink?"

"I'd love a beer, if you've got one."

I stood in her kitchen. My gaze lingered over her body. She had lost weight since I'd seen her last. Her luscious curves were less distinctive. Her clothing floated over her body instead of hugging the soft flesh. Desire ran through my body as it always did when I was near her. I stood rooted by the kitchen table. If I touched her, I would ruin the very reason she let me in.

"Come on, let's go sit on the couch."

I followed her to the living room and waited until she had gotten comfortable. I sat on the opposite end and faced her. I grabbed the beer she had set on the coffee table. I lifted the neck of the cold bottle to my lips and drank half of the contents before I set it back down. It did nothing to quench my thirst for her. I told myself that I wouldn't touch her but I reached out and grabbed her feet and placed them onto my lap. I craved a connection with her.

Her eyebrows rose, questioning my motives. "I can rub your feet without jumping your bones. I told you that I wanted to talk and nothing more."

She nodded and kept her delicate feet in my lap.

"Have you received any more threats?"

She wouldn't look me in the eye. "No."

Fuck. A blind man could tell that she was lying through her teeth. Time to change tactics. She wasn't going to tell me. That's fine; her body language had already told me everything I needed to know. The circles under her eyes spoke volumes. Her luster for life had disappeared, replaced with a hollow look in her eyes. She was running mechanically, not living––simply waiting. I continued to rub the pads of her feet, while my chest grew tighter. Anger threatened to suffocate me. I didn't want to fight with her. This was not of her doing. She couldn't change her circumstances. We were all in a holding pattern.

"I've been working with Enzo lately, helping restore some of the furniture in his shop."

A twinkle shimmered beneath her lashes. "Really? I heard from Candice that you had helped Forrest restore their home. Their house looks amazing. I particularly like the fireplace mantel."

I chuckled. "That was one of the main pieces I had worked on. I was drawn to that piece."

Her surprise and awe brightened her features. "Wow. I am impressed. It's really beautiful. I was surprised to learn that you were so talented with your hands."

"You know very well how skilled I am with my fingers." My voice turned husky.

A rosy hue dusted her cheeks. She was absolutely exquisite.

"What I really wanted to tell you was that I found a pretty piece to work on and I can't wait for you to see it when it's finished."

Her smile stretched from ear to ear. "I'd love to. What about the security business? Have you given that up?"

I shook my head. "Nope. I work at Enzo's when I have down time. That's where I go to decompress. That's how I got roped into dinner at Roselva's. She invited us. I don't expect an answer right now. Just think about it, okay? We are friends, right?" I literally cringed at the usage of *friends*.

"Yes, we are. I can't do more right now."

I looked down at her perfectly purple painted toenails. "I don't like it but I understand. I want you to know that you can always call on me, and I will be there for you."

"Thanks, Mack. I appreciate that."

I nodded. "Come here, Abbie. Let me hold you for a while."

She hesitated but not for long. She scrambled into my lap. She lay in the crook of my arm, her doe eyes searching for answers that I didn't have. I ran my fingers through her hair and down her arm. Her eyes closed and her body relaxed with every swipe. If I could only offer her a minute of escape, then that's exactly what I would do. I would cage the desire to ravage her.

While she lay sleeping in my arms, I found my own peace. I tipped my head back and rested it on the back cushion of the couch. Within minutes, my mind was at rest and the edges of sleep beckoned me.

I woke up with the early morning rays. I haven't had this deep of sleep since she kicked me out. My soul had been refueled. She was the reason for that. Abbie still lay curled up in my arms. I didn't want to wake her so I carefully slid out from beneath her. I grabbed a pillow from her room and placed it under her head. She sighed softly in her sleep.

I wrote her a note before I left. I laid the paper by her coffee machine and noticed her cell phone buzzed with an incoming text. I hated myself for ruining her trust in me but I couldn't ignore it either. I peered at the lit screen. I didn't bother unlocking the phone. One, I didn't have her code and two, the message showed on the screen long enough for me to read it. I snapped a quick picture. The number was blocked so I couldn't trace it.

YOU'RE NOTHING BUT A WHORE AND YOU WILL GET WHAT'S COMING TO YOU. YOU GAVE HIM WHAT WAS MINE. HE CAN'T SAVE YOU, NO ONE WILL.

I sent a text to Holt to make sure he was in place before I left. I had to get the hell out of here before I yanked her from her sleep and made her stay with me. She would adamantly refuse and push me further away. I shut and locked the door behind me.

I opened Holt's car door and hopped into the passenger seat.

"I just saw a text on her phone. I was able to take a snapshot of it."

I handed over my phone for him to read it. I didn't need the picture to tell me what it said. It was forever burned into my brain.

"That motherfucker. Let him try to get her. He won't live to tell about it," Holt seethed.

"He's made us."

"I'd say so. Seems that he has taken to texting because we are here." He scrubbed his face with his hands. "I've kept watch from various spots and not always sitting in my car and I haven't been able to catch even a glimpse of something being off."

"We all have, Holt. You can't guard someone around here without someone noticing. It's a close-knit community, whether or not we are hearing the rumors."

"We are going to have to pull back. Make it seem as though we have given up. I'm going back to the office to get my equipment. I will install a camera above each entry point, with movement detectors. They will be synced to each of our phones. There is student housing down the street. I'll contact the landlord and see if there is an empty apartment so we can set up shop."

"I'll stay put until you get back and we can both go up and get this shit done."

I nodded and got out of the car.

ABBIE 22

I HAD READ THE TEXT AND died a little more inside. I jumped as the phone rang in my hand. Mack's number popped up and I promptly answered. I didn't give a shit anymore about screening his calls. It no longer seemed important. Last night proved that I wasn't over him. He was the calm to my inner storm. When I awoke this morning, I felt more myself. I slept deeply and hadn't woken up once. I hadn't cradled my gun, praying that I didn't have to use it. The only worry that had entered my mind was the fact that Mack would be gone in the morning.

"Hello, Mack."

"Morning, baby. Did you sleep well?"

I had to play this cool. I didn't want him to know how shook up that text made me.

"Better than I have in weeks. Thank you." A smile tugged at my lips.

"It was my pleasure."

"So, what's up?" A slight tremble escaped through my voice.

"Me and Holt are on our way over. We are going to install cameras outside of your doors."

"Mack––" I tried to interrupt.

"Please, Abbie. Let me do this for you. I want you to be able to lay your head down without any fear. You need sleep. You need to be alert at all times and you won't be if you are sleep deprived."

My sigh went through the speaker of the phone. "Okay."

"I'll be there in ten."

I went and cleaned up quickly. I opened the front door in time to watch Mack's formidable frame leading the front. I could barely make out the man behind him. Mack's body took up most of the stairwell.

The stoop wasn't large enough to hold all three of us, so I stood in the doorway.

Mack slid to the right so that the man behind him came in to view. I sucked in a breath, surprised at seeing him again.

"You said that you just happened to be around and heard me that night. Figures that you are one of Mack's guys."

He chuckled. "I didn't mean to startle you that night. Your scream alerted me and I was in the area. I'm Holt, by the way." He held out his hand for me to shake.

I paused, feeling slightly betrayed. "Nice to officially meet you. I take it you already know my name. You probably already know that back in the eighth grade that I had done time in detention."

His throaty chuckle put me immediately at ease. "No, ma'am. Only the necessary information but this detention incident does require further exploration."

I slapped my hand to his and shook it. "It's nice to meet you, Holt." I looked Mack up and down with a snarky smirk. "Come on in and let's get this over with and you guys can quit sneaking around."

Mack and Holt exchanged looks with each other and then stepped inside. They split up. Holt went to the back entrance and Mack worked on the front. I sat in

the kitchen, enjoying the view from underneath my eyelids while I sipped some coffee. The muscles of his arms
pulled against his skin. His shirt rose, showing a slice of
his well-toned abs. I had the perfect view of his wash-
board abs. I licked my lips as my eyes traveled up his
torso. When I met the devilish grin, I promptly averted
my gaze. He kept right on working as though he had
never caught me undressing him with my eyes. He even
added a little whistled tune. *Ugh!* He was a damn tease.
How long were they going to take?

Holt walked into the kitchen. "I'm finished. Mack,
you about done?"

"Yep, just about."

"I'm going to head back to the office. It was nice meeting you, Abbie."

"Thanks, Holt."

"I'm not far behind you. I'm going to make sure the
system is in working order before I head out."

He waited until Holt had disappeared from his sight
before he shut the door and advanced in my direction. I
sucked in a breath when his breath tickled my neck.

"Let's test this baby out," he said with a wicked gleam
in his eyes.

His hips were in perfect alignment with mine.
"Mmhm," I managed.

"Abbie, go out the door so that I can test the system."

He chuckled as I shook myself from my lustful stupor.
I strode to the door with wobbly legs. I stood in front
of the door not entirely sure what I was supposed to do.

"Perfect. Your beautiful image just popped up on my
phone. Let's try the back door."

I sashayed to the back, feeling like a temptress. Two
could play this game. When I was out of his sight, I took
my top off and tossed it over the couch, along with my

bra. I stepped out the back door and waited. I stood there for a minute, making damn sure that he had gotten an eyeful before I headed back inside. I waited for him to say something. When he didn't, I stepped back inside to pick up my shirt and bra. *So much for being a temptress.*

I squealed when Mack caught me from behind. I didn't put up any kind of fight. I wanted his arms wrapped around me. I needed him more than I needed my next breath. His lips tasted my flesh and I was in heaven.

"You taste sweet. I want so much more."

"Then take it. I'm yours," I said breathlessly.

He growled as he used his teeth and tongue to forge a path up and down the side of my neck. His rough hands covered my breasts. He lightly pinched my nipples. My head swam and my limbs went heavy. He turned me so that I faced him. He brought my chin up with his fingers and covered my mouth with his. He hungrily devoured my lips. I reached my arms around his neck and pushed my body closer to his. His hands grabbed my waist and pushed me away. His rejection was like a bucket of ice water.

"It's all or nothing, Abbie. You can't have it both ways." He walked toward the door and turned around. "I——"

He simply shook his head and shut the door softly behind him. I stood there, half-naked and more vulnerable than ever. I should have run after him but something stopped me. I slammed my arms through my shirt and tossed my bra in the hamper. I had some serious thinking to do before I chased after him.

The bar would be at fire code capacity. Broken Down was playing. It would be a welcome change of pace. Between the music and the patrons, I wouldn't have time to think. I knew I wanted Mack and even loved him. But, was it the forever kind? That I couldn't answer. I was living my life without him and it was miserable at best. That right there should've solidified my answer but it didn't.

As the night wore on, I found myself looking for Knox. He hadn't showed up tonight. I missed his solid presence. Marie showed up, presumably to see whether he was here. We chatted and she stayed for a couple of songs and then jetted. She gave some flimsy excuse about wanting to watch a new episode of some show on TV. *Liar!* I blew her an air kiss and sent her on her way.

The night turned out to be awesome for the cash register; for me, I was tired. All I wanted to do was go upstairs and soak away my troubles. I shut off the lights and locked up. I started to climb the stairs when I was forcefully pulled backward. I landed hard on my back and my head bounced off the floor. I lay there, stunned, with the breath knocked out of me. A heavy boot planted itself on my chest. I started to panic when the weight of his foot pressed down harder. I hadn't caught my breath from before. I started to wheeze when the boot finally lifted off my chest.

The body that belonged with the foot crouched over me.

"I told you I was coming. You're mine, angel."

I opened my mouth to scream and he stuffed a bar towel in my mouth. I took a deep breath through my nose, trying to calm myself enough to think of a way out. Instead, a putrid smell entered and it was lights out.

MACK 23

WE SPENT ALL MORNING SETTING up. The landlord had offered us the only remaining apartment. He said that it would be quiet for the next week before the students started filtering back in. Most of them had gone home for break. Only a handful of students remained in the building. That worked well for us. We wouldn't have to explain our sudden appearance. College kids were as nosy as the elderly. The only difference was that I had patience for the elderly not the college kids. They annoyed the fuck out of me.

We set up some pretty uncomfortable lawn chairs and our makeshift desks––otherwise known as folding tables. One lonely air mattress leaned up against the wall. One of us would be here throughout the night. The only downside was that there were no existing windows that captured the storefront of the bar. The bedroom window offered about half of the sidewalk leading up and that was about it. We kept our laptops up and keyed into both cameras outside of Abbie's apartment. The only good thing about this apartment was that it was only a stone's throw away from the bar.

While Abbie worked, we monitored the cameras. They showed no movement throughout the course of the night. Knox slipped out on a sub run and Holt was taking a catnap while I kept a running loop of Abbie's bare breasts from this afternoon. I still can't believe that I had the balls to walk away from her. It had been the stupidest decision that I had ever made. It was true, I wanted more from her. I was tired of being pulled into her bed, only to be thrown out until next time. At one point, a relationship with those conditions was what I sought. Unfortunately for me, I couldn't exist with a romp here and there. *God, I was a sorry sack of pussy.*

Knox blew through the door and a delicious aroma followed him in.

"Damn, man. Those subs smell good. Where did you go? You weren't gone long." My stomach growled.

"Right down the street. Subs on the Side or some shit like that. All I know is that my nose located the place and it was packed."

"Hope they taste as good as they smell," Holt chimed in.

"I could probably eat roadkill at this point. I'm so fucking hungry."

I snatched the bag from Knox and dug for one of the subs.

"You better leave me the turkey, fucker," Knox threatened.

"I'm taking the Italian. I don't care what you meatheads fight over."

I took a healthy bite and mumbled, "This is either really good or I am really hungry."

With their mouths full, both Holt and Knox answered their agreement.

I set my alarm on my phone just in case I fell asleep. With a full belly and not much going on, the probability was favorable that we all would.

I woke with a start when the shrill alarm sounded. It

was two in the morning. She would be closing down the bar. I would give her an hour for her to go up to her apartment. They were busy tonight and the cleanup would take longer than usual. I fired up the sleeping computer and stared at the black screen, willing it to catch her movement. I got up and stretched, moved around, did some jumping jacks, trying to rid my mind and body of sleepiness.

"Keep it down, you lumberjack. You are ruining my beauty sleep." Holt sounded groggy.

I jumped harder just to spite him. I'm not sure what the hell he found to throw at me but it bounced off my chest and hit the floor with a clacking sound. I flipped my wrist over to check the time on my watch. Shit, it was now quarter past three. There should have been some movement caught. There was no way that she was still down in the bar. I checked the cameras and sure enough, no movement had been recorded.

I hollered to Holt and Knox. "Wake the fuck up. Something's wrong."

They both bounded up, fully alert. It was the military's finest training.

"Holt, you take the back of the apartment, and Knox and I will start at the front. Let's move out."

We exited the apartment complex and ran as fast as we could. Holt veered to the left while we stayed straight on the sidewalk. About a half a block from the storefront, we took a crouching walk with our guns pulled out in front of us. There was no element of surprise coming in the front. The lower front of the bar was all windows. We would announce our presence as soon as we crossed in front of the first window. It was a chance we had to take. Hopefully Holt would get in unannounced and could get the element of surprise and change the stakes of the game.

I silently motioned for Knox to cover my six while I tried the door. It wasn't locked. Hell, it hadn't been shut all the way either. The bar was pitch-black. I slowly opened the door and slid through quietly. I waited a beat for my eyes to adjust to the dark. I strained my ears, listening for any sound. *Fuck.* There was only silence. I took out my flashlight and positioned it underneath the handle of my gun. I swung back and forth, canvassing the bar. I looked through every door and nook. Absolutely nothing. I heard footsteps coming down the stairs. A beam from a flashlight caught my eye. It had to be Holt. Knox came through the door. Our three beams of light lit a small area of the bar.

"Find anything upstairs?"

"Nothing."

"Fuck, where is she?" I shouted.

I stopped when my eye caught something dark on the floorboard next to Holt's foot, right in the center of his flashlight beam.

"Don't fucking move an inch, Holt."

I stomped over and bent down. I angled my flashlight, illuminating the spot more. I stuck my finger in the darkened spot.

"Blood," I confirmed for the guys.

I stood and spun around, keeping the light trained on the floor. I walked the path toward the door. I only found one other speck inside the bar, right over the threshold. I used my hand to wave the others to follow closely behind. I looked around the sidewalk in front, looking for a fucking needle in a haystack.

"Fuck. Which way did he take her?" I growled. "Holt, you take the left. Knox you go straight across to the other sidewalk. I'll go right. Any sign, holler."

I walked carefully and examined every inch of concrete. We were losing precious time. I shouldn't have pulled everyone off her detail. I wanted to flush him out and I sure as fuck did and screwed all of us—especially Abbie—in the process. *What if I didn't find her in time? No, I would. I had to.* I was about a block down from the bar when I scored another hit. I hollered to my men. They scrambled up and flanked my sides. With the three of us searching together, we covered that much more ground. We found one more droplet of blood right out in front of our complex. *Motherfucker. He was right under our noses the whole time.*

I punched in the landlord's number.

"How many residents are still in the building?" I boomed.

"Who the hell is this? Do you know what time it is?" he hollered into the phone.

"It's Mack and I don't give a shit what time it is. Answer the fucking question and now."

"I don't know. As long as the rent gets paid, I don't care what the fuck they do."

I punched the End button. He wouldn't be any help, that cocksucker. He'd get a size thirteen up his ass after all this was said and done.

"Holt, you take the top floor. Knox, you got the ground, and I'll take the second floor. Look for blood before we start busting down doors. Text before we think it's the right door. We will all meet there before we go in."

I hit the up arrow for the elevator. I wanted to check and see whether there were any droplets of blood. Sure enough there was one.

"Change of plans. Knox, you take the stairwell to the second floor. I'll take the elevator and Holt, you continue to the third via the stairs."

The elevator doors dinged open. The fluorescent lights cast an eerie glow down the hallway. I turned immediately to the right, my eyes cast toward the floor. They shifted to the left and right of the wide hallway, always searching. I went all the way to the end and found nothing. My phone pinged. It was from Knox; he was at the other end of the hallway, standing in front of one of the apartments. He had copied us both so I sprinted down and stood next to him. I put my ear to the door. At first I heard nothing and then I caught a muffled voice. I looked down and sure enough, another droplet of blood had fallen right outside of this very door.

Holt stood next to us, battle ready. Knox got into position to kick the door in. I flanked behind and to the right and Holt to the left. I would go in first, then Holt, and finally Knox. This isn't like TV: the door doesn't get knocked open in one kick. It should take no more than two the way that Knox was built. His powerful leg went up and smashed the door open on the second try. I rushed through with my gun drawn.

ABBIE 24

MY HEAD WAS POUNDING. *WHAT the hell had happened?* I tried to reach up and rub the back of my head. My arm wouldn't move. I tried again, with the same result. Panic set in as I remembered. *Shit, shit, shit.* This wasn't supposed to be happening. *All of my training and preparation flushed right down the shitter. I can't fight my way out of this.* My legs and arms were strapped down and taped to what looked like a kitchen chair. I picked my heavy as lead head up from my chest and checked out my surroundings.

I was in someone's kitchen. The only furniture seemed to be the chair that I was tied to. Everything else had either been removed or never furnished. The linoleum had yellowed with age. A slow whirring sound came from the fridge. The door out was to my left. It wasn't close enough to scoot to. It would be pointless. It's not like I could open it even if I got close.

Nothing was familiar. I hadn't been dragged up to my apartment and this wasn't the bar. My heart thumped wildly in my chest. *Oh God.* No one would know that I had gone missing until tomorrow evening when the bar was supposed to be open. By then it would be too late.

I flinched when I heard a voice.

"You are finally awake. I'm so glad. Now we get to

play."

I looked up and into Travis's manic face. I should've listened to my gut after I had seen him at the store. He had given off a weird vibe and I didn't give the feeling any credit. I completely underestimated him. I had thought that he had gotten the hint back at the bar but all I had done was spur him on. Maybe if I played his game, I would live long enough to get out of this somehow.

"What do you want from me, Travis?"

I had made my voice as docile as I could.

"What is mine, of course."

"What is yours?"

"You. You are mine, Abbie."

I took a deep breath in, making my headache worse.

"Untie me and you can have me." I pleaded with my words and my eyes.

"You are already mine. Before I untie you, I need to teach you a lesson."

The gleam in his eyes terrified the piss out of me. My body trembled and tears escaped from my lids. He wasn't going to untie me. He was going to kill me as I sat strapped and defenseless to this chair.

"Please, untie me. I'll do whatever you want." Another sob escaped.

I hated to sound weak but I was. I was fighting for my life the only way I knew how.

"STOP!" he screamed at me. "You've had your chance and you blew it. I asked you nicely multiple times and each time you were more rude."

He produced a sharp butcher's knife from behind his back. The steel reflected the light from above. I squinted and turned my head to the side. He grabbed my chin and forced me to look at him.

He brought the knife to my neck and applied enough

pressure to break the skin and draw a single drop of blood. The droplet of blood slid down my neck as the tears flowed down my cheeks. My body trembled as I sobbed.

The blade shallowly scratched along my neck until he reached the neckline of my shirt. In one swift motion, he had sliced my shirt open. He hacked at the shirt until it lay in tattered shreds on the floor. I closed my eyes when he walked behind me. Not being able to see what he planned to do terrified me more than watching his madness. I felt the cold tip of the blade bite into my flesh. Not hard enough to cut my skin. It was merely a warning for me to remain quiet and still. I didn't dare breathe. He slid the blade beneath the clasp of my bra. The knife easily sliced through the lace. He brushed the knife up my back and cut each strap that lay over my shoulders.

I was completely bare from the waist up. The urge to cover my breasts after he cut my bra away gnawed at me. My arms twisted in their constraints but all it did was solidify that I was at his mercy.

"You are so beautiful. It was your red hair that caught my eye. I couldn't keep away from you." He walked around to face me. "You ruined everything. I've been watching you for some time now. Long before we entered the bar and you were ready to kick my friends and me out. When I touched your hand, I felt a spark. I know you felt it too because that night you invited me up to your apartment." He reached out and grabbed a lock of my hair, twirling it around his fingers. "So soft and silky." He pulled the strands tightly against my scalp as he lifted them to his nose. He sniffed loudly. "Smells even better."

It hit me as he stood there, ogling my half-naked body: I could be at his mercy physically, but I controlled where my mind went and how I reacted to his cruelty. I may not walk out of here but I would not grovel for my life.

I closed my eyes and told God that I was ready and to make sure that my mom and father were waiting for me at the gates. It was time for me to be reunited with my family. The fragrance of my father's cologne washed a calming wave through me. I couldn't explain it and I would never try. He filled my head full of memories. I sucked in a breath as fresh tears rolled down my cheeks. He had gifted me an image of my mother holding me in her arms as an infant. Her whispers of love washed over me as I gazed up at her adoringly. Until that moment, I hadn't realized how much I had missed her. Her last words were "Live for me, baby girl. Your daddy will take good care of you as I look down upon you from heaven." The memory of my mother made me sad and long for her more. I was even more ready to go.

My father's voice whispered through my mind. "It's not your time, baby girl. Your mother and I are standing beside you. We will help you get through this. Do not give up. FIGHT!"

The last word was shouted through my mind. My eyes popped open. He was right. I would see my parents again but not yet. I glared at Travis. I wasn't ready to die and for as long as I could, I would fight to live.

"You're nothing but a lowlife piece of shit that preys on women. Why don't you untie me and see if you get an ounce of flesh from me?" I goaded.

"Shut up. I am in charge, not you. I'm going to make you scream before I kill you." He waved the knife around maniacally.

"Go ahead and kill me because I wouldn't want your worthless hands touching me ever again. WHAT ARE YOU WAITING FOR," I screamed at him.

"I'm going to drive this knife straight into your heart and watch as your life slips away. If I can't have you, no one can."

"Then do it, you sniveling coward. You are nothing but a needle-dick pussy."

"You fucking whore." He raised his arms and lunged for me.

I kept my eyes opened and grinned as I leaned all of my weight to the side, tipping the chair over. With nothing to thwart his momentum, he crashed to the floor. The knife bounced on the floor and flung out of his reach. I lay on my side, my shoulder aching from taking the brunt of my fall. I racked my brain for my next move. I flung my head in the direction of the door. I couldn't quite see what was happening but I could hear a pounding. In a split second of the first pounding, a second blow blew splinters of wood past my head.

Travis scrambled to reach the knife but a blur of muscle grabbed me––chair and all––and whisked me to the other side of the room. I recognized the muscle as Knox. I looked over to where Travis lay. Sitting on top of him was Mack. Mack used his fist to pummel Travis's face until he was almost unrecognizable. I didn't scream for him to stop. No, I silently encouraged him to continue.

Knox freed me, and I walked calmly to where the butcher knife lay. I picked up the sharp blade. I gently placed my hand on Mack's shoulder. He immediately stopped landing blows. He stood and went to wrap me in his arms. I gently placed my hand on his chest. I didn't want comfort just yet. I had unfinished business. I knelt on my knees, raised my arms over my head, and heaved the knife straight into Travis's heart. His body jerked from the force and blood gurgled out of his bruised and discolored lips.

"I didn't give up, Daddy. I'm not sorry it ended this way, but I couldn't let him live."

Mack picked me up and cradled me to his side. "It's over, baby. I've got you."

Holt slipped his shirt off and handed it to me. I looked up at him and smiled. "Thank you."

I gave my statement, slightly spinning the truth as to how the knife ended up in his heart. I could go to jail but I didn't think that I would. I had three witnesses to verify my story. Those minor cuts from the knife, my tattered clothing, along with a busted lip and tape abrasions along my wrists and ankles, said far more than what I gave to the police. They told me not to leave town. That was hilarious, because where would I go? I had my life back and I planned to live it here in town. I was no longer afraid of living or death. I knew what waited outside this apartment as well as in heaven. I had the best of both worlds, where people loved me from both sides.

The paramedics had finished cleaning out my wounds. I had gotten lucky with my head wound. There was no need for stitches. They released me into Mack's care. He walked me back to my apartment. I sighed with relief that I no longer had to hide in fear.

I turned toward him. "Please stay the night. I don't want to be alone yet."

A slight tremble went through my body and suddenly I felt cold.

"Shit, let's get you into the shower and warm you up."

I nodded and followed him to the bathroom. I watched him turn on the faucet and constantly check the warmth of the water. As steam built up in the bathroom, my teeth began to chatter.

"Okay, baby. I'm going to let you get undressed. I'll be right outside if you need any help."

"Thanks."

I wasn't ready for him to see me naked. I wanted to wash away Travis's lingering effects. I stood underneath the spray of the water, washing any traces of my ordeal down the drain. I let the tears fall when it finally hit me that I had killed him. I'd like to blame it on temporary mental and physical insanity but I had known exactly what I was doing. I had consciously made the decision to end his life. If I hadn't, I would have been in constant fear for the rest of mine. I know life held no guarantees. However, I assured my safety from him. He could no longer hurt me or any other woman who decided to reject him. I'd plead my case in front of God when I arrived: until then, I was surprisingly comfortable with the decision that I had made. *I'm not sure what kind of person that made me or how it would shape me in the future.* I'd have to wait and see.

I stepped out of the shower and dried off. I felt stronger and mentally free.

"Mack, do you mind grabbing me a shirt to sleep in, please?" I asked through the half-opened door.

"Any particular one?"

"Whatever you grab is fine."

His arm reached through the door, with the shirt dangling from his fingers. I plucked it from his fingers and slipped it over my head. It was baggy and reached just above my knees. I looked in the mirror and chuckled. It was one of his that he had left here. On the front, *Do or Die* was printed in bold black lettering. How fitting.

I walked out and faced Mack. He stood strong and

fierce, with an unreadable mask in place.

"Thank you."

"Come, let's get into bed."

He picked me up and cradled me in his strong hold. He gently laid me onto the bed. I scooted up to the pillow and watched him take his clothes off. *What a work of art.* His imperfections made him more perfect. With his boxers still on, he scooted in next to me. He pulled me to his side. I rested my head over his beating heart.

As I drifted off to sleep, I murmured, "I love you. Stay with me forever."

"Forever, my Ruby. I love you. Now sleep."

MACK 25

I RAN MY FINGERS THROUGH HER hair, down her arm, and back up again. My fingers never broke contact with her soft skin. I had come too close to losing her. Her swift thinking had bought her enough time for us to find her. She had saved her own life by staying alert and never giving up. I was in awe of her strength and perseverance. There were highly trained men who would have succumbed in similar bleak situations.

I wondered whether she would hold strong come morning. Taking a life wasn't easy, even for someone such as me. I would forever remember my warrior kneeling before her enemy and showing no mercy. He was already within an inch of his life after my pummeling and for her mental sake, I'm grateful that she landed that fatal blow. If she hadn't, she would always be guarded and looking over her shoulder. It gave her the closure she needed to move on. I drifted off to sleep with her snuggled into my side.

I startled awake quickly, checking to make sure that Abbie was still softly sleeping by my side. The side of her bed was cold and empty. I threw the covers off and searched for her.

"Abbie," I called out.

"On the couch," she returned.

A soft glow from the table lamp was the only source of light. Abbie sat tucked in the corner of the couch with her knees bent to her chest. I sat next to her and pulled her to me.

"Want to talk about it?"

"A nightmare woke me up. It had felt so real. This time it was Travis who plunged the knife into my chest," she whimpered.

"I'm not going to tell you that you will get over this because you won't. You will relive it a thousand different ways. What I do know is that you made the right call. No matter what your conscience is trying to tell you. The only thing that I regret is that I allowed him the opportunity to get to you and that it was you and not me who killed him. I love you, Abbie, more than life itself. Without you, my existence would simply be a shell."

She squeezed her body closer. "I love you too, Mack. Do you understand why I pushed you away? I didn't have a choice. I couldn't bear it if something had happened to you." Her sad green eyes stole my heart. "How can you still be with me? I coldly ended a person's life and I don't regret it."

"I have more blood on my hands than you can ever imagine. You have nothing to be ashamed of. You aren't a lesser human being because of this. You defended your life and if he hadn't done this to you, he would have chosen another woman. You rid the world of a sick and twisted predator. That doesn't make you a killer. You did this out of self-preservation. You have too much heart and love for those around you. Do not define yourself from this one action."

She rose up and gave me the most tenderhearted kiss. "Thank you for saving my life."

"Sweetheart, you saved mine long before you saved

your own."

I hadn't sugarcoated that either. She had saved me. She gave me a new look on life that wasn't desolate. A life I didn't think that I had deserved. She was the hero of my story.

ABBIE 26

WITH MACK'S URGING, I TOOK time off from the bar. I let Eddy and the rest of the crew handle the bar. I almost felt human. Days after the abduction, I couldn't get out of my pajamas. I would relive the same scene over and over again. The nightmares continued but I expected them now. I no longer woke up screaming in the middle of the night. Mack started sleeping over a couple of nights during the week. The nights that he wasn't beside me were when I had the worst nightmares. He took the edge off and never looked at me differently. He treated me the same as he always had. I think that was the part that helped me heal. Marie and I were on shaky ground only because I couldn't take the sympathy in her eyes. We would get back to normal but it would take time.

Saturday rolled around and I was lying in bed, fretting over Roselva's dinner tonight. I didn't know her or her family that well. I was worried what would come out of her mouth. She wasn't one to beat around the bush. She said what she was thinking and it could be both a blessing and a curse for those around her.

"Come here, you worry wart."

Mack's deep voice was like a smooth whiskey heating my blood. I scooted closer to his side and lay my head over his strong beating heart.

"You will do great tonight. Just be you. They are going to love you."

"I don't understand how you became part of the family."

He chuckled. "Why wouldn't I be? Everyone loves me."

"You're such an arrogant ass."

"And you love my arrogance and my ass."

"Sometimes I wonder why."

He rolled us over. I giggled at his mock outrage.

"You'll pay for that comment."

"I hope so."

His large, callused hand caressed my side, down to my hips and back up. The tips of his fingers brushed the side of my breast. I moaned, already intoxicated from this man. One touch and I melted. He lowered his face and melded his mouth to my lips. His tongue lazily danced with mine. I took in a lungful of much-needed air. He kissed along my jaw and ventured down my neck. He used his tongue and teeth over my chest, sending sweet, torturous electrical shocks straight to my clit.

His lips touched my nipple with tantalizing possessive-ness. His fingers met my wetness, making me squirm more. His lips moved to the other breast, where his tongue circled my hardened peak. His fingers gently massaged my clit, sending currents of desire through me. He kissed his way down my stomach to the swell of my hips. With each kiss, he whispered his love. My lips parted; a soft moan split the silence in the room. My senses reeled as if short-circuited.

In a split second, his fingers left my wet center. I watched, delirious, as he aligned his bulging shaft to my entrance. I dug my fingers into his waist and pushed him home. I wrapped my legs around his hips and pushed him deeper. His body cleansed my guilty conscience and his love mended every crack, making me whole again.

"Greedy," he moaned as he thrust in and out.

I didn't protest. I was greedy and heady with lust. With each thrust, my impatience grew to explosive proportions. He drove in and out and I cried out for release. His thumb circled my clit and I shattered into a million glowing stars.

I lay in his arms, still glowing. "Move in with me."

His body moved partly over mine.

"I thought you'd never ask," his lips whispered against mine.

Mack brushed his thumb over the knuckles of my hand throughout the short drive to Roselva's. The knots had formed in my belly as I got ready. They intensified the closer we got. My breaths became shorter. I felt as though I was going to hyperventilate. He parked along the curb.

"Abbie, look at me."

I twisted my body so that I faced him. He leaned his large frame over the center console and pressed his lips to mine, caressing my mouth more than kissing it. The kiss was as tender and light as a summer breeze. Instantly, the knots transformed into a burning desire and an aching need. He pulled away and left me feeling weak.

"You coming?"

His deep chuckle breezed through the opened door. I had been so wrapped up in my desire that I hadn't realized that he had already exited the car and had my door open.

"That is not even funny." I glared at him.

"You should see it from my end. Your tongue is still hanging out of your mouth. You might want to correct that before we go in."

I swatted him on the ass, jolting him toward the house.

"Kinky. That can be arranged."

"You really are a pain." I giggled, secretly excited about what might be in store for later.

The door opened with a whoosh before we could knock.

"Took you long enough to get out of the damn car. You know, it's a public place. I thought about calling the law to break you two apart."

She grabbed Mack as though he wasn't built like a brick house and crushed him to her smaller frame. He bent down and wrapped his arms around her fuller figure. She rose up and kissed him in a motherly way on his cheek.

"I'm glad you came, son."

His beaming smile was all that I needed to see to have all of my nervous tension washed away.

While I was holed up in my apartment, Candice came over and we had a long talk. She dropped hints about Mack's past. Roselva had been smitten with Mack and loved him like a son. Her love was what he had desperately needed and somehow she saw that. My respect for her grew exponentially.

She opened up her arms for me, and I rushed in. She enveloped me in her fleshy arms.

"My sweet child." She held me at arm's length and studied me. "I see the fire in your eyes. You did what most of us couldn't do when faced with a hard decision. God would never condemn you for that and neither will I. I am proud of you and the strength it took." She tenderly kissed one side of my cheek as her meaty fingers pinched the other side. "Now, get inside so we can eat."

She opened the door and we filtered in. For an Italian home, the place was eerily silent. Growing up in Marie's household taught me that your outside voice was the same as your inside voice. You could scream your fool head off and still not be the loudest one in the room. She shuffled us through the house and into the large open kitchen. From every corner and free space in the room, family and friends shouted, "Surprise!" My hands flew to my face and covered my mouth. Marie scrambled from her hiding spot, with Lia hot on her tails. They both slammed into me with gusto.

"Momma Rose invited us all here today to show you that we love you."

I squeezed them both heartily. "I love you guys more then you'll ever know. I'm sorry for being so distant."

"Don't worry, girl––nothing has changed. Now, let's enjoy your freedom celebration."

My eyes widened. *Did she just make a joke at my expense?* I laughed so hard that I started to cough. She slapped me on the back roughly.

"Good one. We are back on even ground. Damn, girl, you pulled out all the stops with that one."

"I know, right? I'm awesome. You can thank me later."

I giggled. All the pieces that I had been missing had fused themselves together. What Mack couldn't mend, Marie did. Roselva had outdone herself: she had managed to take a simple dinner and bring it to a homecoming with everyone I loved and who had always supported me. All of my employees and even some of the regular customers had shown up. The Broken Down members had even set up in the backyard. I spotted Curtis in the corner, with his arm slung around––presumably––his wife's shoulders.

I walked up to him and thanked them for coming.

"Abbie, meet my wife Joanne."

"A pleasure." I shook her hand.

"We wouldn't have missed this for the world. Glad you are back."

Once the words had come out of his mouth, he cringed and Joanne slapped him upside the head.

I moved through the crowd until I found Roselva. I hugged her tightly. "Thank you for bringing such a wonderful gift to me."

"I've known you since you were a baby. Your dad used to ask me to watch you now and then. Not often enough, I must admit. You've always been family––be sure to remember that."

Unshed tears shimmered in my eyes. "I'll help you set out the food."

"A wonderful help you'd be. Lyle," she shouted into my ear.

I jumped at her booming voice.

Mack snagged me around the waist. "Still nervous?" he whispered in my ear.

A toothy grin adorned my face. "Not at all. I love you."

"Love you too. We better set the table or Momma Rose is going to tan our hides." He nibbled my earlobe.

"Cut that out." I swatted him away.

He chuckled and we went to grab the dishes.

After dinner, we went out to the yard. Mack and I sat on the wooden swing and watched Riley and Lia running after one another, squealing. There were so many people that I couldn't wrap my head around it. I had always believed that it was my dad and me. Thanks to Mack, he showed me that I had a very large family ready at my beck and call.

Broken Down had begun to play right after dinner and hadn't taken a break yet. Brett seemed determined to play every song I liked. Mason had even taken a turn singing some of the bluesy songs I loved.

All of a sudden, a hush came over the crowd. Roselva's prosthetic breast had been tossed onto the amp. It jiggled like Jell-o with the last lingering strums of the bass. Roselva walked over to the stage and picked up her prosthetic and shook it at Lia.

"It has to stay in the fridge to keep its shape. It is not a toy and I'm the only one who can throw it around. You got me?" The gleam of delight twinkled in her eyes.

Lia hung her head while she had been reprimanded. Gia ran up and grabbed her arm.

"Sorry, Momma Rose. I won't throw it again," she apologized too sweetly. A tiny devilish smile twitched at the corners of her innocent mouth.

The crowd dissolved into fits of laughter, which brought Lia's smile brighter. That child was going to be hell on wheels when she grew up.

The band picked right up where they had left off as though a molded breast had never graced their speaker. I had always heard of the rumors but had never believed them until tonight.

"I'm glad that thing wasn't thrown my way."

I laughed until a stitch in my side made me groan. "I've got two very attached ones that you can play with later."

"Why wait? Let's get out of here."

"Fantastic idea."

We said our good-byes an hour later and headed back home.

MACK 27

I SCREECHED TO A HALT AND raced Abbie up the stairs. She had already unlocked the door by the time I had caught up to her.

"I'm going to tie you up and have my way with you."

Her eyes got as big as saucers. "And I'm going to let you."

A wicked gleam quickly replaced the fear that had snuffed out the twinkle.

I had gotten so excited about the thought of tying her up that I didn't even think of the possibility that it would be a bad idea. Hell, it hadn't been that long since she had been kidnapped. The fear in her eyes was like a swift kick to the balls. Which I deserved for being so selfish and callous.

She was in her closet, rummaging around, when I walked into her room. She popped out with a silly grin. "You'll have to use these winter scarfs. I don't have anything else."

She gently placed them in my hands. I was dumbfounded that she really wanted to go through with this.

I fisted the thick threads. "Another time. I shouldn't have said anything."

She turned her back to me. Her delicate hands bunched the hem of her shirt and lifted it achingly slow over her head. The curves of her body were lit in a soft glow. Shadows danced across her back and she stepped out of her pants. Her fingers skillfully unclasped her bra. She turned to face me with her arms crossed, covering the silky swell of her breasts. She grinned mischievously, dropped her hands, and sauntered toward the bed.

I watched her perfectly heart-shaped ass still clad in her skimpy panties sway back and forth as she climbed toward the headboard. My dick pushed painfully against my jeans, threatening to bust free and claim what was his. *Down, boy. We haven't even begun.* I groaned when she lay on her back with her arms spread wide. Her fingertips barely grazed the cold metal of the frame. I tore the clothing from my body, not caring how clumsy I looked. I desperately needed skin-on-skin contact. I wanted to tear across the room and ravage her. Instead, I forced myself to calmly walk to the side of the bed. I picked one of the softer scarfs and tied a slipknot around the post. I wanted her to be able to free herself if being bound became too much. I gently wrapped the material around her feminine wrists.

"If you want me to stop at any time, say stop, and I will."

"Is stop our safe word?" she teased.

"I'm being serious. Do you agree?" My voice took on a stern tone.

"Yes. I agree," she answered breathlessly.

My girl liked me to talk rough to her. I stored that little nugget for later.

I placed my lips where the scarf covered her dainty wrist. I grazed my fingers along her soft flesh as I continued to the other side. I kissed the other wrist when I was finished. She moaned her acceptance. I stood at the edge of the bed, gazing at every dip and swell of her body. Her sweet, musky aroma drifted toward my nose and sent tiny jolts of electricity to my balls. My dick hardened more, reaching for her pussy.

I climbed between her powerful thighs. I ran my fingers from the heel of her feet to the inside of her thighs. Her moans deepened the closer I got to her center of pleasure. I skimmed my knuckles over the crotch of her panties. They were soaked. Knowing that she could be this wet so quickly turned my insides out with desire. I lowered my head and licked the thin, lacy material. Her taste was unlike anything I've ever experienced. Her lavender soap mixed perfectly with her sweet musk.

My tongue made a path up her stomach to the swell of her breasts. I moved my mouth over her dusky nipple, pulling the tight bud flat against the roof of my mouth. I swirled my tongue around the hardened peak before I paid equal attention to her other breast. My fingers continued their light caressing over her panties. I was rewarded with her soft moans.

My lips burned a path from the base of her neck up to the lobe of her ear. I bit down gently on the fleshy part of her ear. I lifted my head to brush my mouth over her parted lips. My tongue darted inside her warmth. My tongue explored the hot slickness of flesh inside. Her tongue melded to mine and drove a wave of heat to my throbbing dick.

I slid my fingers beneath her panties and into her slick folds.

She tossed her head back, breaking the kiss. "Ahh," she cried out.

"Fuck, I can't wait any longer." The deep baritone of my voice scratched against my throat.

"I'm ready, Mack. Take me before I lose my mind."

I jimmied to my knees, moved her panties to the side,

and positioned my cock to her opening. I rolled my hips and plunged inside her hot center. *Shit!* Her pussy clamped around my cock and pulled me in deeper. I held still, relishing the way her inner muscles wrapped around my dick like a heated blanket. The walls of her vagina squeezed my dick and I lost my control.

My thumb traced circles around her clitoris as I drove in and out. Her pussy pulsated around my dick as we both chased ecstasy. She began to move her hips in tandem with my thrusts. I plunged harder as she rode my cock. I groaned and released my seed. I didn't stop until her cries were spent and her body loosened its grip. I gently slid out of her and climbed off the bed. I released her wrists, lovingly kissing the palm of each hand.

I curled up behind her. "Were you frightened at any time?"

"No. If I had been would have said stop. I only felt love."

I felt her smile through her words as they slid like warm heat over me. I pulled her closer and nuzzled the base of her neck and whispered a kiss. "If you ever want a career change, let me know. I'd be honored to have you be a part of the team."

She giggled. "You'd be the first one to know."

I squinted from the bright fluorescent lights. I ran my fingers through the neck of my shirt. *Shit, it was as hot as a damn sauna in here!* Fucking jewelry stores gave me the willies. Glass cases lined every available floor space of the store. My big-ass frame kept ramming into the corners. My hips were going to be bruised when it was all said and done. I was going to ask Forrest to come with me. I'm glad I decided against it. I would never hear the end of his shit.

"Hello, can I assist you with anything?" the sales clerk eagerly asked.

Her plastered-on smile was large enough that I could see her molars. Shit, her teeth were bright as a fresh winter's snow. *Did she greet all her potential customers this way or was I the only asshole?*

"I'm looking for an engagement ring."

She stepped from behind the current display case and motioned for me to follow her. I stopped when she easily slipped between two cases toward the back of the store.

"Do you know what kind you are looking for?"

"Nope. I'll know when I see it." At least I thought I would.

I bent over the clear glass and peered down at several beautiful rings but nothing caught my eye.

"Would you like me to pull any of them out?"

"No. Almost every ring in this case looks alike. What else do you have?" I stood to my full height.

She had to tip her head back to look at me. "Let's take a look at another case."

She moved down one case to the left. Again, I peered over the glass. They were beautiful but still nothing that I could picture Abbie wearing. She would be happy with anything I picked out but I wanted something with more flair. Abbie wasn't a flashy woman but she had a zest for life and I wanted something that would capture that. I shook my head to answer her question.

A ring in the next case over had caught the corner of my eye. "I'd like to see what is in that case." I pointed to the right.

She moved into position. Once again, I leaned over the

glass, careful not to put my meaty paws on top. I didn't know how fragile the glass was; with my luck, I'd break the damn thing. *Go in for one ring and come out with a whole case of them.* In the top left corner of the case sat the ring for Abbie. I didn't ask how much. The price wouldn't deter me from buying it. The ring was perfect. Excitement from her potential reaction ricocheted through my chest, accelerating my heartbeat.

"Bag her up. That's the one." I pointed to the precious gem.

Her eyes lit up as if it were Christmas morning. Maybe it was, for her pocketbook. I got the feeling that she worked on commission. By the looks of her shocked face, I'd guess that gave her a hefty bonus.

"Excellent choice, sir. This piece is stunning and will look gorgeous on her hand."

I nodded. "Thank you."

With the petite bag hanging from the tips of my fingers, I walked triumphantly to the car. Now all I had to do was come up with the perfect way to ask her. I sat in the car, worrying over how to do this. *Did I take her out somewhere nice and put it in a glass of champagne, like a normal douchebag?* Nah, that wouldn't work. *Fuck.* I started up the car and stewed over it the rest of the way home. I passed Enzo's shop and slammed on the brakes. *Perfect.* I sent a quick text to Abbie and let her know that I'd be working late tonight.

I walked through the shop doors, strutting around like a damn fool. I couldn't stop the grin from permanently attaching itself to my lips. I officially looked like a jackass.

"Hey, Mack. It's been awhile," Enzo greeted me.

"Yeah, I got something special in mind. Do you mind if I work in the back?"

"Nope. I have to head back to my real job. Tommy is here if you need anything."

"You should quit that banking crap and do this full time."

"Not yet. Soon."

"Oh, I forgot to let you know that I wanted to buy that cigar-looking box. It's going to be a gift for Abbie."

"I picked that up cheap. I don't even know why I did. You can have it. On one condition?"

I raised my eyebrow. "What's the condition?"

"I want to see the finished product."

I laughed. "I can do that. Thanks."

I said a quick hello to Tommy before I headed to the back. I set my stuff down and grabbed the box. Enzo had all of the things that I needed so I set right to work. I fitted the inserts and stepped away. I walked over to the cabinet and snatched the woodburning kit. I plugged it in. While I waited, I watched a bunch of You Tube videos. *Woodburning for dummies!*

I picked up a piece of scrap wood and practiced. If I hadn't, I would certainly screw up the wood. Drawing was not my forte but a tree I could handle. I made sure to use each tip in the kit to see what would work the best. *Shit*. Pain radiated up my fingers when I went to switch out the tip. I shook my left hand. *That was flipping hot.* I grabbed a pair of pliers and switched the tips that way. With some repetition, I got the hang of it.

I moved the box in front of me and began to burn the lines into the wood. I crinkled my nose as the smell of a campfire and burnt popcorn intensified. I worked well in to the night, not stopping until it was completely finished. The hardest part to move past was the tiny imperfections but I think they added more character. The roots of the tree were on the bottom front of the box. The tree rose from the tip of the top lid to the top. There was a perfect leaf-shaped tip in the kit. The outcome turned out better than I had predicted.

I opened the lid and the top insert was designed to fit some of her favorite jewelry. If you took out the insert, the bottom of the box was lined in black felt. That was where her gun would be hidden. I placed the insert back inside and dug out the ring box I had stashed in my pocket. I gently stuck the ring in the middle of the ring holder. I shut the lid and locked the box.

"You were going to sneak out of here without showing me the finished product."

I hadn't even heard him come in. The door wasn't exactly silent. It made a tiny screech when you opened and closed it.

I laughed at being caught. "Sure was."

He walked over and stood beside me. He picked up the box and examined each side. He even tipped his head over and peered on the bottom. The lines around his eyes crinkled. He was pleased so far. He unlocked the box and looked inside. The ring sparkled in the light.

"This is your best piece yet." He placed the box in my hands and squeezed the top of my shoulder. "She is going to love both."

"Thanks. Let's hope she says yes."

"I don't think she will have an option to say no."

"Damn skippy." I chuckled and walked out the door.

I held one hand on the box and one on the steering wheel. I couldn't afford to have anything happen to this box before I got home. As soon as I walked through the front door, I searched for the perfect hiding spot. I walked through the whole apartment and I couldn't find a satisfactory one. *Guess I was proposing tonight. Leave it to me to have nothing planned.*

I sat on the couch, with two glasses of wine filled to the brim. The jewelry box sat between the stems. I got up and paced the room. She would be here any minute. My mind raced along with my heart. Nervous energy flitted through my limbs and made my stomach queasy. *What if she said no?* I'd have to move out of state from the humiliation. *Could it be too soon? There was a possibility that she wasn't ready to get married.*

I was all in. I wanted that signed document that proclaimed her as mine. I wanted her to drop her maiden name. My name was the only one she needed. I wanted babies. *Wait, not yet.* I still wanted to walk around the apartment buck-naked and wake up in the morning, making love to my wife first. I wasn't ready for midnight feedings and the disruptions to our sex life. I was selfish enough to want her all to myself for a while.

The back door opened and my Ruby walked through like a fresh rain on a warm summer's evening. Lavender fields permeated the room, making me lightheaded. She always had that effect on me.

I captured her smaller hand in mine. "Have a seat, beautiful. I have a gift for you."

Her genuine smile was infectious. "Shall I close my eyes?"

"It's not necessary. It's already sitting in front of you."

Her forest-green eyes drifted over the box. Her lips parted as she ran her hand along the wood. She looked over at me. "Mack, did you make this?"

A sheepish smile took shape. "Yes. I did."

I promptly knelt before her. I sandwiched her left hand

between both of mine.

Her right hand rose and covered her luscious lips.

"Abbie. I've walked along a darkened path most of my life. My parents left to my own devices. I don't know if I'll make a great husband like your father was to your mom. However, I will make sure that I try every day to make you proud of me. You have been the calm to my storm and the sunshine to my darkness. I am a better man since you have come in to my life."

"Get to the good part, Mack," she interrupted.

I laughed, knowing that I had been rambling and not getting any of this right.

"Will you, Abbie James, marry me and love me even though I am the most undeserving man on earth?"

I opened the lid of the box.

Her eyes opened wide and tears shimmered. "Mack, we both deserve a life full of love. You are the only one who has ever made me see that."

I took the delicate ring out of the box and slipped it onto her ring finger.

She nodded fiercely as her tears slid down her cheeks. "Yes. Yes, I'll marry you."

She peeked down at the ring sitting elegantly on her slender finger and gasped.

"It's a ruby. Oh my goodness. It's stunning. How did you find this?" Her breaths came in short pants.

"If I tell you, I'll have to kill you." I grinned. "Seriously, though, the lady said something about platinum and the finest quality of diamonds and a non-heated gem. I have no clue what all of that means. All I know is that it had your name written all over it."

She placed her hands on the sides of my cheek. The tips of her fingers were ice-cold but her palms radiated heat. "I love you and this gorgeous ring. It's perfect."

"Let's drink to your yes."

We lifted our glasses.

"Mmm. This is the wine that will give me an orgasm in my mouth and leave my body wanting more. Excellent choice."

A wicked grin spread across my face. "I think I can out-do that bottle of wine."

She giggled. "I'd like to see you try."

I picked her up and hauled her curvy frame to the bedroom. I had to make this one the best one yet. Even in the nursing home saddled with a forgetful mind, she would remember this night.

EPILOGUE

I WAS THE LUCKIEST SON-OF-A-BITCH THIS side of the tracks. I couldn't tell you the type of dress she wore or how her hair was styled. What I can tell you is that the green of her eyes bore a resemblance to the green canopy of the Amazon. The air was dense with a heavy richness from her lavender body wash. I could taste the fragrant flowers on my tongue. The vibrancy of life flowed through her shimmering eyes, energizing every cell in my body. Her love radiated in waves as she walked toward me.

Lyle placed her hand in mine. She had asked him to give her away. He had lost his shit over her request.

"I know where to properly dispose of your body if you hurt her." He stared me down.

"Won't be necessary." I winked.

I stood before my beautiful bride with our hands intertwined. Her silky skin was the exact opposite of my callused ones. I stood in awe that she had said yes. There was still time to back out. I prayed that she had no regrets. I wasn't easy to live with. I monopolized most of her free time. When I was away for work, I longed to be home with her. I craved her more than a meth junkie. Forrest and the rest of the crew called me pussy-whipped and I didn't disagree. I was and I loved every minute I spent with her. We could fight like cats and dogs but the make-up sex was reason enough to fight.

The damn justice better hurry the hell up so I could kiss my bride. Her bright ruby-red lips taunted me. My focus was mainly spent trying to keep my dick from tenting my pants. Momma Rose sat in the front row and I know she would call me out for being a horny teenager.

"You may now kiss the bride," the justice of the peace announced, loud enough for me to come out of my Abbie fog.

Halla-fucking-luyah. I dove in and devoured my bride right in front of everyone. She tasted of her favorite red wine and chocolate: such a heady mixture. We walked down the outdoor aisle and straight into the reception. We didn't want posed pictures; we requested that the photographer capture in-the-moment ones. We were making our own traditions. We decided to book the entire Oliver Inn and Winery. So far it had been worth every penny. She wanted to get married here and I wanted only the guests we invited to the wedding on the grounds. I booked it for the whole weekend so that we could honeymoon with our family and friends. I think we had shut down our little town. Just about everyone who lived there was present.

The afternoon had been perfect. Not a cloud in the sky to taint my wife's day. This was all for her. I was only along for the ride. We decided on a middle of the afternoon wedding so that our guests could enjoy some wine tasting and other activities that the inn was known for. We had the inn set up a buffet of finger foods and tons of wine. Hell, they could keep the reception going well into the night if they wanted.

Broken Down was set up in the corner on the dance floor. I could hear them tuning up their instruments before they began to play. We had no clue what their set would be. We decided to let them do their thing. They were an incredible band and played a little bit of everything. Why hinder talent?

Forrest strode over and bro hugged me. "You clean up real nice. Congratulations."

"Thanks, man. You covered up your ugliness well."

He grinned and enveloped Abbie in a warm, brotherly hug. "You look stunning."

Her grin radiated. "Thank you, Forrest."

I heard Riley from across the room, shouting my name. I turned in her direction. She ran at full speed, zigzagging around everyone who got in her way. The flower dress was adorable on her. The skirt flew up and covered half of her face as she navigated her way to me. Her little body shot in the air, landing in my outstretched arms. I trapped her legs in my arms just in case her flailing legs decided to kick me in the junk. She had a tendency to do that from time to time.

I smiled into her excited cherub face. "Hey there, princess. Where's the fire?"

Her giggles sent tingles of joy to my heart. "Thewe's no fiwe, silly. I wanted the fiwst dance."

I hugged her tightly to my chest and winked at Abbie. "You got it, princess. The first dance goes to you."

I set her down on the floor. She placed her tiny hand in mine. You could barely see her little fingers. I walked over to Brett and told him what I wanted. We walked hand in hand out to the dance floor. The band had begun with a slow ballad. She stood on top of my sneakers while we did a slow circle. All of a sudden, the beat changed. Her eyes lit as bright as fireworks on the Fourth of July. She jumped off the tops of my feet. She threw her hands out to the side, signaling for me to get off the stage. I laughed heartily, knowing full well she wanted to show off her dance moves. The band played a wicked electric guitar riff of the "Gangnam Style" song. She flounced around the dance floor as though she were riding a pony. Her little arms and legs were flying all over the place. I marveled at my little showstopper. Everyone gathered around and cooed and clapped, egging her on.

When the song finished, she ran over to me and hugged me as tightly as she could. She huffed and puffed her thanks. She pointed her little finger at me and rose to her toes. I squatted to her level. She grabbed my face with her chubby little hands and smacked my lips with a kiss.

"Wuv you, Unci Mack." She grabbed Forrest with her wide, innocent eyes. "Daddy I'm hungwy. Can we eat?"

We all laughed at her sweet and demanding self.

Brett dedicated the next song to Abbie and me. I turned to my wife and placed my hand over hers, stealing her away from Marie. We walked toward the dance floor. I twirled her into my arms when the slow ballad began. I crushed her body to me. I loved feeling her curves against mine. Her body fit nicely against mine. Tonight, the material of her dress put entirely too much space between us and yet I could still feel the heat pulsating, filling up the empty space. I waltzed her around the dance floor.

I whispered in her ear, "I'm having a hard time sharing you. I want you all to myself. I can't wait for the inn to be full of your cries of ecstasy."

Her flesh broke out in goose bumps. "You are so raunchy."

I molded my lips to hers, affectively smothering the rest of her words.

She broke the kiss. "An hour tops and I'm all yours."

"I can deal with that."

The song ended and I tipped her back. As I brought her

back, my lips met hers with a scaring kiss that lasted long after we parted.

Shortly after, we left our guests. I tore her out of the reception like a madman on a mission. The skirts of her dress blew behind her as we ran to our room. I opened the door to our suite. I picked her up and carried her over the threshold.

"You didn't have to do that. My legs aren't broken."

"Yes, I fucking did. That's one tradition I won't break."

I let her place her legs back on the floor. I turned her so that her back faced me. Her shoulders were bare. I lowered my lips to her shoulder and kissed a path along her back to the other. I unzipped her dress, letting it fall to the floor. She stood in the middle of the fabric as it lay around her feet. I bent at the knees and licked my way down her spine. She shivered with excitement. I wrapped the sides of her panties in my fingers and tore through the flimsy material. I caressed her heart-shaped ass. I nibbled each fleshy cheek. I stood, grabbed a fist full of her fiery locks, bringing her around to face me.

"You drive me crazy. I am punch-drunk with love. Everything about you makes my dick hard. I can't think of anything but being buried deep inside your warm pussy."

"You're such a charmer. I couldn't imagine my life any other way. Now, finish what you started," she demanded.

And I fucking did.

OTHER BOOKS

ABOUT THE AUTHOR

Jenni Bradley lives in Florida, with her husband, three daughters, three dogs, one cat, and four horses: pretty much a small, funny farm where there is never a dull day. She enjoys riding most days. The other days are usually met with hard dirt and a happy horse.

You can find Jenni online at www.jennibradley.com to find out more, plus news on upcoming books.

You can also find Jenni on Facebook at
www.facebook.com/Jenni-Brad-
ley-145317865832928/

Goodreads at
www.goodreads.com/author/show/14237910.Jenni_
Bradley

www.ingramcontent.com/pod-product-compliance
Lightning Source LLC
Chambersburg PA
CBHW071902220626

47052CB00002B/170

* 9 7 8 0 9 9 6 6 8 3 8 3 8 *